AN ENEMY'S REVENGE

The sun crowned the horizon. Already, the mild chill of the night was giving way to the warmth of the new day. Warmth that would soon transform the prairie into hell on earth.

One-Eye Jackson set his rifle down and slowly drew his bone-handled knife. His eyes glittering with the lust to inflict pain and suffering, he hunkered and smiled. "Well now. Where to begin?"

Nate focused on a pillowy cloud high in the azure vault.

"I aim to whittle on you a while. Maybe cut off a few fingers and toes. Or how about your nose? Your wife won't think you're so handsome then, will she? Not that she will ever see you again."

#51
WILDERNESS
COMANCHE MOON

David Thompson

LEISURE BOOKS NEW YORK CITY

Dedicated, as always and forever,
to Judy, Joshua, and Shane.
And to Kyndra, Josh's special princess,
and to Tori and Brian.

A LEISURE BOOK®

March 2007

Published by

Dorchester Publishing Co., Inc.
200 Madison Avenue
New York, NY 10016

ISBN 0-8439-5713-1

Visit us on the web at www.dorchesterpub.com.

COMANCHE MOON

PROLOGUE

There were two of them. They were white, and they came from the north. The horses they rode were draft animals that doubled as mounts when the need arose. The third horse was a pack animal with a sway back they had picked up on their way west.

Both men were in their middle years. Both wore homespun shirts and pants that had seen a lot of use. As had their battered hats and scuffed boots. By their clothes and their sun-browned complexions, they were men who spent a lot of time outdoors.

For days the pair had seen only grass, grass, and more grass. Trees were as scarce as hen's teeth, water only slightly less so, which explained why, when they came to a meandering ribbon of blue amid the green, they promptly made camp for the night. Plenty of jerked venison was in their saddlebags. But they were not all that interested in eating.

The two men were excited.

"It's better than we dared hope, Elmer," said the oldest. He had a few gray hairs at the temples and a cleft chin.

The man so addressed also had a cleft chin, as well as a similar nose and brow. The similarities suggested they were siblings. "So much land! And as much as we want, ours for the taking!" declared Elmer with almost childish glee. "Ten years from now we'll have farms bigger than some states."

"Just the two of us?" Hiram said. "That will be some feat."

"Shep will help," Elmer said. "Between the three of us we'll become as rich as John Jacob Astor. He did it with fur. We can do it with corn and wheat. We'll have our own little empire."

Hiram chuckled. "An empire now, is it? Where do you come up with notions like that? I'll settle for pleasantly prosperous. For being able to provide for our families. That's the important thing." He sank his teeth into a piece of jerky and hungrily chewed.

"The trouble with you is that you don't think big enough," Elmer said. "There's nothing to stop us. There's no law on the books to keep us from claiming as much as we want."

"Hush, you infant. Don't jinx us with talk like

that," Hiram scolded, only partly in jest. "Remember, Pa used to say that when a thing seems too good to be true it probably is."

"There you go again." Elmer's gestured at the sea of grass. "Haven't you got eyes? It's endless and empty."

"In a hundred years there will be so many folks living west of the Mississippi River, a body won't be able to spit without hitting a neighbor."

"We won't be around to see that," Elmer said. "Which is just as well. I like people as much as the next person, but I like my privacy more."

Hiram, too, encompassed the plain with a sweep of his left arm. "Is this private enough for you?"

Elmer nodded. "There's not another soul for a hundred miles."

"Make that five hundred, not counting Bent's Fort."

They smiled and laughed, and then Elmer made a comment that sobered them. "And not counting Injuns."

For a while the brothers chewed and did not say a word, until finally Hiram shivered slightly and said, "This night wind sure gives a man a chill, even in the summer."

"Sure does," Elmer agreed.

"We haven't come across any sign of redskins, you know," Hiram mentioned.

"Not hide nor hair," Elmer said. "I reckon all the tales we've heard weren't true. It can't be as bad as everyone claims or we'd have run into some of the devils by now." He patted one of two flintlock pistols wedged under his belt. "Not that I'd be all that afeared if we did. I can hit a melon nine times out of ten at twenty paces."

"Don't brag on yourself," Hiram said. "It's unseemly." He bit off another piece of jerky. "I figure another two or three days ought to be far enough. Then we'll head back to Bent's Fort and send word to Shep. While we wait for him and our families, we can build our soddies."

"It will be grand!" Elmer predicted. "The Beecher boys, kings of the prairie."

Hiram snorted. "We're plow chasers, plain and simple. That's all we've ever been, it's all we'll ever be. Whether we own a hundred acres in Indiana or a thousand acres out here."

"You think too small," Elmer said. "Five thousand is more to my liking."

"One man can't work that much," Hiram said. "Hell, three men couldn't. Your yearnings have outstripped your common sense."

Elmer opened his mouth to reply but closed it again when a wavering cry pierced the night to the west, ululating on the wind like the wail of a wandering specter. "Do you reckon that had four legs or two?"

"It was a coyote," Hiram said, "not a painted savage."

"I reckon all this talk about Injuns has me a mite spooked."

"It's all this wide open space," Hiram said. "It

makes a man feel downright puny." He leaned back against his saddle and stretched his long legs out. "We'll get used to it, though, once we've settled in and lived here awhile."

"Sure we will," Elmer said. He, too, leaned back, placing his rifle within easy reach. "What I don't get is why there aren't more people doing what we're about to do."

"Blame the government and the newspapers," Hiram said, "with their nonsense about this being the Great American Desert. We've seen for ourselves. This soil is as rich as any back home."

"Richer," Elmer said.

Hiram tore a handful of grass out by the roots and sniffed the roots. "Fertile as can be. Perfect for crops. We'll start with corn and wheat, and take it from there. The excess, we'll sell."

"And there will be a lot of excess," Elmer predicted. "We'll have dozens of hired hands to help out."

"There you go again, putting the cart before the horse."

"We'll be the first," Elmer said. "In our own way we could become famous."

"Such foolishness," Hiram said. "Men don't become famous for farming. They become famous for fighting. Like Jim Bowie and Davy Crockett did at the Alamo."

"They're as famous as can be and always will be," Elmer said.

"Nothing is ever forever. Always is only as long

as folks remember, and memories are fickle."

The pair stayed up until near midnight, talking. At last they turned in and slept the sleep of the blissfully ignorant.

There were five of them. White men called them red men, and they came from the southwest. They rode as if they were one with their mounts.

They called themselves the Nemene. Everyone else called them something different, a name that instilled stark fear at its mere mention. They were as widely feared as the Apaches, as fierce in their defense of their territory as the Sioux.

They were not on the warpath. They were hunting. They had come north after buffalo, the shaggy brutes on which their people and so many other tribes depended for food and for many of the articles they used and wore.

They rode in single file. Relatively short in stature, they had high, sloping foreheads, and alert, piercing eyes. Their hair was worn parted in the center, and braided. They were naked from the waist up. Fringed leggings and moccasins sufficed. They bristled with weapons: bows and arrows, lances, war clubs, knives, and ropes.

Their horses were as fine as horses anywhere. Animals with speed and stamina. God dogs, the Nemene called them. Which mystified those who did not understand how much the horse meant to them. Before the coming of the horse, the Nemene toiled hard to survive, and were no more exceptional than other tribes. After they acquired the horse, their toil lessened, their lives were made easier. But more than that, the Nemene became the lords of their domain, able to strike with lightning swiftness and seemingly be everywhere at once. God dogs, to them, was apt.

The Nemene were divided into bands. The five riding north were Wasps. To those who were not Nemene, that meant nothing. To those who were, it meant a lot.

The five came to a ribbon of a stream and turned east, searching for sign of the great beasts they sought. Presently they came across fresh tracks but not the tracks of buffalo. They came across the tracks of three horses heading south, and a tense excitement gripped the five warriors.

The hooves of the three horses were shod.

"White men," Nocona said. He was the tallest of the five, uncommonly so for his people.

"Here?" said Pahkah, he of the crooked nose. His surprise was shared by the others. Never before had they encountered whites so far into their hunting territory.

The tracks led south, so they turned south. Buffalo were forgotten. The whites were more important.

Soko, the oldest by a few years and the best tracker, hung down over the side of his horse, an elbow and a knee crooked to keep from sliding off. "Only two. The third horse carries heavy packs."

"Only two?" Pahkah sounded disappointed.

"We know what we must do," Sargento said. His body was a block of rippling sinew.

A grim air came over them. The whites were invaders and the Nemene treated all invaders the same.

Pahkah bitterly remarked, "The whites are locusts. They are everywhere. They push in from the east. They push in from the south. Now these two, from the north. Where there are two, more will follow."

No one said anything. Their sentiments, when it came to white men, were similar. It was more than hate. It was a deeply felt seething resentment, easily provoked.

The Nemene had heard what the whites did to other tribes. How the whites had driven the tribes from their lands, or wiped them out with bullets and blood, or brought disease that wiped them out even more effectively than the bullets.

The Nemene knew little of the country to the east of the father of rivers. But they did know that at one time other tribes called that country home, and now many of those tribes were no more, or had been forced west of the great river, and the whites now overran that country from end to end.

A sage among the Nemene once compared the whites to a thunder head on the horizon about to swoop in and engulf the Nemene in a deluge. "There is nothing we can do to stop the storm from coming," he had said.

But that did not mean the Nemene had to suffer

the same fate as those other tribes. They were a proud people. They bowed to no one. They surrendered to no one. Maybe other tribes had not been able to resist the whites, but the other tribes were not Nemene. The Nemene would succeed where those others failed.

"Why are the two whites here?" Soko wondered aloud.

"What does it matter?" Sargento responded. "It is enough that they are."

"The whites are many things we do not like, but they are not stupid," Soko said with the patience that came from being older than they were. "They do not do things without a reason."

Sargento's scowl darkened his swarthy features. "You might not think they are stupid, but I do. They are poor hunters, poor trackers, and poor fighters. Only in numbers are they great. Were it not for their numbers, they would be nothing."

"Say what you will," Soko said, "but the reason they are here is important."

"They hunt buffalo, like us," Pahkah suggested.

When Soko did not say anything, it was Nocona who prompted him by asking, "Share your thoughts. I am interested." It was Nocona who had organized the hunting party.

"Why do they hunt this far south?" Soko asked. "Have all the buffalo to the north died?"

"That is silly," Sargento said.

"No. He is right." Nocona stared at the tracks

of the shod horses. "There are plenty of buffalo for the whites to hunt to the north. Why come this far when there was no need?" He looked at Soko. "I would hear more."

"I see several paths," Soko said. "It could be they are on their way to join the whites in Texas, but no whites have ever come this way before. It could be they are buckskins, exploring, but the whites who wear buckskin live off the land, like we do, and do not need packhorses." Soko paused. "It could be they look for a place to live."

Had the ground opened up and swallowed them, the other four warriors would not have been as shocked.

Pahkah started to laugh, as if it were a great joke, then caught himself. "You believe that is what they do?"

"This is our land," Sargento said.

"When has that ever stopped the whites?" Soko countered. "To them, all land is theirs. Did they not take the land of the Cherokees, the Creeks, the Seminoles? Did they not take the land of the Chickasaws and the Choctaws?"

"But not *here*," Pahkah insisted. "It is too far from their villages of stone and wood."

"Their villages are not as important to them as our villages are to us," Soko said. "Remember what we have been told. It starts with a few. Then, if something is not done, more come, and ever more, until there are as many as there are blades of grass. By then it is too late to oppose them."

"We must not make the mistake others have," Nocona declared. "We must not let these whites or any others build a lodge on land the Nemene have long roamed."

"There are only two," Sargento said. "It will be easy."

"Two we know of," Soko said. "What if there are others? What if these two are part of a larger party?"

"You are saying we should not slay them?" Sargento growled.

"I say we should watch them awhile," Soko suggested. "Once we know they are alone, then do with them as you want."

"I say we kill them as soon as we catch up to them," Sargento said.

Pahkah looked to Nocona. "What do you say?"

"Soko's words are wise," Nocona said.

The fifth warrior, called Howeah, had not said a word the entire debate. He did so now. "I agree. If I dropped my knife in a rattlesnake den, I would look to see how many rattlesnakes were in the den before I stuck my hand in to get the knife."

Sargento glowered. But then, Sargento nearly always glowered. His temperament made him hard to get along with. Even his fellow Wasps believed he was more bloodthirsty than was normal, although none said so to his face.

The issue decided, they followed the tracks of the whites. It was late in the afternoon when

Howeah, whose eyes were those of a hawk, spied wispy tendrils of dust on the horizon.

"I hope we find they are alone soon," Sargento remarked. "My fingers itch to slit their throats."

Twilight shrouded the plain three days later when Hiram and Elmer Beecher brought their weary mounts to a halt in the middle of a hollow some forty yards in circumference.

"This is as safe a spot as any," Hiram said. "No one can spot our fire."

Brush along the west rim provided the fuel. Elmer took his fire steel and flint and hunkered. Kindling was everywhere. A handful of dry grass, a few puffs of breath, and a tiny flame blossomed into their campfire.

Hiram had shot a rabbit earlier. He skinned it and cut the meat into chunks while Elmer filled a pot with water from their water skin and added a cup of flour and bits of chopped onion. The stew that resulted was more broth than bite, but after days of nothing but jerky, it was a feast. They ate slowly, savoring every mouthful.

The pot was empty when Elmer leaned back and patted his gut. "That was fine. I am in heaven."

"You and your stomach." Hiram grinned. "No wonder women think the way to win a man is with food."

"In my case it was," Elmer said. "My Hannah is the best cook I ever came across. Better than Ma, even."

"Now, now," Hiram chided. "Your missus is as sweet as sugar, but Ma is the best cook ever."

"I will be sure to tell your wife you said that."

"Abby would be the first to admit she's not a wizard with the stove," Hiram said. "The first biscuits she made me were so hard I used them to pound nails."

The brothers chuckled.

Elmer filled his tin cup with steaming hot coffee, sipped, and gave a contented sigh. "How much farther, do you reckon, before you're satisfied?"

"We need a spot with trees and water. We can't build cabins without timber, and the water goes without saying."

"We'll find a spot," Elmer said. "There has to be one."

"The last timber we saw was along the Platte," Hiram reminded him. "Maybe we should build there. It's not much, as rivers go, but it flows year-round, and there's plenty of game and fish to be had."

"It is close to the trail to Oregon country," Elmer said. "It wouldn't be like we were in the middle of nowhere."

"And closer to Bent's Fort and any supplies we might need."

"Our wives would like it better there than here," Elmer added.

They were quiet awhile, and then Hiram said, "What do you say? Are we in agreement? Do we write to Shipley and tell him we have changed our minds? That we like the notion of a cabin along the Platte River better than a little house on the prairie?"

"We are in agreement," Elmer said.

"Then tomorrow we head back to Bent's Fort," Hiram said. "After we rest up some, we'll scour the Platte for sites."

They were in good spirits when they fell asleep, but the same could not be said when they woke up. Hiram, as usual, was the first to sit up, stretch, and admire the dawning day. Astonishment tinged with dismay brought him to his feet with his rifle in his hands.

"Elmer! Wake up! The horses!"

Always slow to rouse from slumber, Elmer mumbled, "What? What are you on about?"

"Our horses are gone!"

"They're what?" Elmer sluggishly rose on his elbows and gazed in the direction his brother was gazing. With an oath, he shot from under his blankets as if fired from a catapult. "Where are they?"

"How should I know?"

"But I hammered in the stakes myself," Elmer said. "I tied the knots. The horses couldn't pull loose."

Hiram bent over one of the stakes and held the length of rope still attached to it so his brother could see. "These were cut. Someone snuck in during the night and stole them right out from under our noses."

"Without waking us up?" Elmer was incredulous.

"We're stranded afoot."

"Maybe we can spot them," Elmer said, and ran toward the hollow's rim. His brother shouted for him to stop, but Elmer paid no heed. The steep incline slowed him, but he pumped his legs harder and gained the top.

"Damn it, wait!" Hiram bellowed.

Elmer shielded his eyes from the glare of the rising sun and anxiously scanned the prairie in all directions. The only sign of life was a few birds flitting about in the near distance. "Damnation."

Hiram churned up the slope and stopped, puffing for breath. "That was stupid, running off like you did. You know as well as I do what those cut ropes mean. We have to stay on our guard."

"I'm fine, aren't I?"

There was a buzzing sound, and an arrow caught Elmer high in the right shoulder. The jolt spun him half around. He stared at the feathers in disbelief. Then the agony struck.

"Elmer!" Hiram cried.

Another ash shaft tore through Elmer's left thigh even as a third transfixed Hiram's right arm. Hiram dropped his rifle. Frantically backpedaling, they threw themselves down the slope. Hiram rolled, clutching his right arm to his side. Elmer hit on his left thigh and cried out. At the bottom they shakily rose and faced the rim.

Unlimbering a pistol, Hiram looped his other

arm around Elmer to help him stand. "We're in it deep, brother."

"Don't I know it," Elmer gasped.

Shoulder to shoulder they retreated toward the charred embers of their campfire. No arrows sought their flesh. No war whoops rent the air.

Elmer was struggling to stay conscious, Hiram trying in vain to glance in four directions at once.

"Where are they?" Elmer winced. "Why don't they show themselves?"

"They're in no hurry. We're not going anywhere."

"I wish we could pull these arrows out," Elmer said.

Hiram looked at the shaft that had pierced his bicep. Blood stained his shirt, and the stain was spreading "They're good, whoever they are."

"How do you figure?" Elmer asked. "They missed our vitals."

"They weren't trying to kill us," Hiram explained. "They want us hurt and weak so they can take their sweet time finishing us off."

"Sweet Jesus." Elmer's face was as pale as paper. "I hadn't thought of that." He gripped his brother's shirt. "I don't want to be tortured."

"That makes two of us."

"We should run for it before we lose too much blood. Then it will be too late."

"It's already too late," Hiram said, and nodded.

Mounted warriors had appeared on the rim. Two to the north, one each to the east, south, and west. The warriors had arrows nocked to sinew strings but made no attempt to use their bows.

Elmer pointed his flintlock but did not shoot. "Which tribe are they, do you reckon?"

"Comanches."

"Oh God," Elmer said. "Oh God, oh God, oh God, oh God."

CHAPTER ONE

He was white, but there was much about him that was red: his shoulder-length black hair, his beaded buckskins, his moccasins. The sun had burned him darker than most whites, with the result he looked almost red. But the beard gave him away. The beard, and his green eyes, twin emeralds that swirled with the untamed currents and haunting eddies of the wilderness.

He was white, but he was dark. He was tame, but he was wild. He was at home in two worlds, that of the white and the red, yet he lived in neither. He had carved his own niche, a niche for him and his loved ones, and he would live no other way.

His white name was Nate King. Nathaniel King, to be specific, after the apostle in the Bible.

His Indian name, a name bestowed on him years

ago by a Cheyenne warrior but now the name by which a dozen tribes called him, was Grizzly Killer. Of all the white men who ever lived, of all the red men who ever were, he had slain more grizzlies than any other. Not by choice. Not by design. In the early days of the beaver trade, when grizzlies were as thick as ticks on a Georgia hound, whimsical fate had thrown him into in the path of grizzly after grizzly. It had been fight or die, and he was fond of breathing.

White by birth, Shoshone by adoption. Two worlds, the white and the red. Two worlds at war with one another. Two worlds that refused to get along. Refused to extend the hand of friendship, preferring instead the bloodied fist of battle. Mutual loathing was the order of things, so that many thousands of whites hated the red race for no other reason than they were red, and many thousands of red men and women hated whites because they were white.

Two sides, always at each other's throats. Two sides, despising one another so fiercely, they waged relentless conflict. Two worlds that had one trait in common: their deep-rooted hatred.

Nate King hated neither. He had lived as a white and he had lived as a red, and he had discovered the two were much more alike than either was willing to admit. They shared similar hopes, similar fears. Strip away the different clothes and the different customs and they were, at their core, people. Ordinary people.

Nate considered himself ordinary. Others might disagree. He had sacrificed the prospect of becoming an accountant at a prestigious New York firm to travel west. In the Rocky Mountains he began a new life, that of a free trapper. When the demand for plews peaked, he remained in the mountains. They had become as much a part of him as his blood. He was one of the first to become known as a Mountain Man, a hardy new breed that dared any peril in the pursuit of personal freedom.

Nate did not mind being called that. He lived in the mountains, and he was a man. A man with a devoted wife, a lovely Shoshone named Winona who had borne them two children, a son, now married, and a daughter.

Nate's wife was the reason, on this scorcher of a summer's afternoon, with the blazing sun the only splash of color in an azure sky, that he reined his dusty bay to a stop on a low rise and gazed down on the destination he had ridden ten days to reach. "There it is," Nate said to the bay. "A lot of bother to go to, if you ask me, but if it makes her happy, then the bother was worth it."

Built on the Arkansas River, Bent's Fort was best described as an adobe castle. The siblings who built it, William and Charles Bent, along with their other brothers, bestowed the name. Their partner in the enterprise, Ceran St. Vrain, bestowed his aristocratic manner and a flair for business. The Bents and St. Vrain were typical of most whites in that their purpose was to make a lot of money trading with the red man, but they were not typical in that they did not look down their noses at their customers.

Far from it. William Bent had been adopted by the Cheyenne, just as Nate had been adopted by the Shoshones. Bent had taken another page from Nate's book and married a Cheyenne maiden. A chief's daughter, no less.

The fort, which was not a military post and was not manned by soldiers, was neutral ground. A place where warriors from sundry tribes came to barter. Often the warriors were enemies. Anywhere else, they would fly at one another with the urge to count coup roaring in their veins. But not at Bent's Fort. It was understood that any tribe that broke the truce would be banned, and the fort was the source of dearly desired articles tribes could not obtain anywhere else.

Nate had been amazed the first time he set eyes on the trading post. The years had not diluted his amazement.

It was huge. The outer walls were more than three feet thick, rendering them impervious to bullets and arrows, and close to fifteen feet high. The front and rear walls extended one hundred and forty feet, the side walls close to one hundred and eighty. Within those walls was room enough for a two-hundred-man garrison and several hundred animals.

The comparison to a castle was not romantic

whimsy. Perched atop the northwest and southeast corners were round towers eighteen feet across manned by lookouts with artillery pieces. Several times a year the field pieces were set off. To celebrate holidays, the Bents and St. Vrain claimed. But they also did it to intimidate the Indians, and it was remarkably effective.

Entrance to the fort was through a wide gate in the center of the south wall. A gate that was kept closed for safety's sake. Near the door was a small square porthole. Those wanting to be admitted had to first show themselves at the porthole under the watchful eyes of the lookouts in the southeast tower and the sentries on the ramparts.

The small wooden slat slid aside at Nate's knock. A ruddy face bristling with a red beard and grimy with dirt and sweat peered out.

"Who are you, then? You don't look entirely white and you don't look completely Indian. But you're certainly not red with those green eyes of yours, or I'm not an Irishman."

"My name is King. I'm here to see Ceran St. Vrain."

"How is that again?" the man said. "Sure it is that Mr. St. Vrain does not personally meet with every rascal who pays us a visit, whether red or white or in between."

"You must be new," Nate remarked.

"Finnin's the name, and yes, boyo, I've been here two months. I intend to be here many more, which is another reason I cannot rush off to do your bidding. I like my job."

"He won't fire you for fetching him," Nate said. "He's expecting me."

"Well acquainted, are you?" Finnin said with ripe sarcasm. "Next you'll be spinning a yarn about supping with him on occasion."

"I've known Ceran a good many years," Nate confirmed. "He and I have shared a table, yes."

Finnin chuckled. "Is that so? And what was your name ag—" He caught himself, and blinked. "Did you say *King?*"

"That I did, boyo," Nate said, smiling.

"You wouldn't by any chance be the gentleman I've heard so much about? The one who brought elk meat last winter when everyone was starving."

"One and the same," Nate admitted. "I was telling the truth when I said that Ceran and I—" Nate stopped. The ruddy face had disappeared. There was a commotion, and a scraping sound as the bar was lifted. He gigged the bay on through.

"Welcome, Mr. King," Finnin said with a bow and a flourish. "Bent's Fort is at your disposal."

"You change with the wind."

"I deserve that. But no, sir, I'm not as fickle as most any female. It's just that I have my orders." Finnin studied him. "So you're the great man. The legend. Up there with Bridger and Carson and Shakespeare McNair."

"My best friend and mentor," Nate said.

"Is that so?" Finnin was genuinely impressed.

"That makes you doubly famous, then. I've heard Mr. St. Vrain mention you. All about how you saved his life once."

Nate went to ride on but Finnin had more on his mind.

"Is it true what folks say, sir? That you've killed more of the giant silver-tipped bears than any boyo since Adam?"

"So rumor has it."

"Humble, are you? Well, that's nice. It truly is. But if you have done only half the things people talk about, you have no cause to make so little of your accomplishments."

"If you say so," Nate said. "But you shouldn't believe everything loose tongues and liquor spill."

"The men who told me about you, sir, were as sober as the two of us are right this minute." Finnin grinned and winked. "Make that you. I might have had a wee dram for breakfast to wash down my mush. And now that I think about it, I forgot the mush."

Nate grinned. He had taken a liking to the fellow.

"Look me up later and you can treat me to a drink," Finnan proposed.

"Since it's your invite, shouldn't you treat me?"

"I'm Irish. Finagling is in my blood. But I'll gladly treat you if you get me drunk enough."

Nate chuckled. "I doubt I'll be here all that long."

A short way in, buildings surrounded an open

square. To the right was the blacksmith shop. Past it, the trading post proper. Along the inside of the west and north walls were corrals filled with milling horses and mules, a few oxen, and not a few cattle.

As usual, the post was awhirl with activity. A large party of traders bound for Santa Fe were buying supplies. Mingling with the traders were settlers, frontiersmen, and friendly Indians: Crows, Nez Perce, a number of Cheyenne, but no Shoshones.

The hitch rail was lined with mounts. Nate tied his bay to the near end. After stretching to relieve a cramp low in his back, he cradled his Hawken in the crook of an elbow and went in. He stopped in the doorway.

The aisles between the shelves were packed with people. The shelves themselves were crammed with every item under the sun, or at least every item hardy travelers venturing into the heart of the unknown would need. Everything from ammunition to jerky to blankets to an assortment of knives. From bolts of cloth to tools, lanterns, and lamps. From harness and bridles to sewing needles, flour, axle grease, shirts, pans and more. A lot more.

The clerks were hard pressed to keep up with demand. Scurrying busily about, they answered a hundred and one questions, or accepted payment.

Nate took one look and promptly turned around. He did not see St. Vrain, which was just as well. The press of human flesh was not to his liking. Backing out, he leaned against a post and debated where to look next.

"I see you made it, Nathaniel."

Only one person called Nate by his given name. Smiling, he turned and held out a large, callused hand. "Ceran. It's a pleasure to see you again."

"Of course it is," St. Vrain said. He was, as always, a fount of suave charm.

The two of them laughed, and Nate said, "Still the same old Ceran. What can I do to repay you?"

"Friends do not help friends for a reward," St. Vrain said. "They do it *because* they are friends."

Nate did not want to seem too eager despite the long ride and his yearning to return home, so he asked, "How is Bill these days?"

"As unflappable as ever," St. Vrain replied. "Half the time he is off with the Cheyenne. He's a lot like you. He has become so much like the Indians, he could almost pass for one. But I must admit that his lovely wife, like yours, is a priceless treasure."

"I'll have to remember to call her that when I get back," Nate quipped. "It will impress her."

"I suppose you are anxious to learn if your shipment has arrived?" St. Vrain asked. "Worry no longer. It has. Two weeks ago. I placed them in a back room for safe keeping. They are quite fragile, and I was afraid something might happen to them." He motioned. "Follow me."

Nate threaded through the press of people in the post. A redwood among saplings, he towered a full head over most everyone else. With his broad shoulders and breadth of chest, he was a living portrait of raw vitality.

"So how is that new valley of yours?" St. Vrain inquired. "The one you relocated to a while back?"

"It's everything we hoped for," Nate answered. "We have a cabin on the shore of a lake. My son and Shakespeare McNair built their cabins nearby. There's plenty of game, and so far we've only had a few encounters with hostiles."

"Only a few?" St. Vrain grinned. "But to be fair, judging from your past descriptions, it's a veritable Eden."

"Anything new here?"

"I'm afraid not. More of the same. More people using the Santa Fe Trail. Which means more customers. More Indians coming to trade than ever before. Which also means more customers."

"I should think that would make you happy," Nate remarked.

"A person can only earn so much money before the rest becomes so much clover," St. Vrain said. "To be honest, I am tired of the long hours, the never-ending work. I relish the thought of spending more time with my family. It could be I am ready to put myself out to pasture."

They came to a door at the rear. St. Vrain opened it and moved along a narrow hall, passing other doors, until he came to the last one on the right. It opened into a storeroom. Crates were piled high.

Ceran St. Vrain put his slender hands on his hips. "Now let's see. Where exactly did I place them? Ah, yes. Now I remember."

There was barely enough space for Nate to squeeze through to a far corner. He was puzzled when St. Vrain abruptly stopped and looked about in bewilderment. "Something the matter?"

"This is deuced peculiar. I distinctly recall placing them on that crate in the corner, yet now they're gone."

"Someone took them?" Nate had gone to a lot of trouble to surprise Winona, and it angered him to think the surprise had been spoiled.

"I don't see how that could be," St. Vrain said. "I gave explicit instructions they were not to be touched." He spun. "Come. We will investigate. I apologize for the delay."

"It's all right," Nate said. But it was not all right, and if anything had happened to them, he would be fit to turn into one of the bears he was named after.

As they came to the main room, the hall door opened and in hurried one of St. Vrain's employees, a thin man with fewer hairs on his head than Nate had fingers.

"Ah. Allan. Just the person I am looking for."

"Sir?"

"Remember the two items I ordered for Mr.

King, here? The items I placed in the back room?"

"Certainly, sir," Allan said.

"They are missing."

"How can that be, sir?"

"That is what I would like to know. They have to be on the premises somewhere. Ask everyone. Find out who moved them. I will be on the southeast tower with Mr. King."

The heat in the square was stifling. Nate squinted in the harsh glare and said, "The tower?"

"Another train of freight wagons was due several days ago. I have been keeping an eye out for them."

They crossed toward the stairs. Jammed as the square was with people and animals, they had to pick their way. St. Vrain glanced over his shoulder to say something to Nate and inadvertently bumped into a burly mule skinner. "Pardon me," he said, and went to go around.

The mule skinner, one of three busy rigging teams to wagons that would soon depart for Santa Fe, shoved St. Vrain and growled, "Watch where you're going, you damn dandy."

"See here—" St. Vrain began.

The mule skinner shoved him again, so hard that St. Vrain stumbled and nearly fell. The reek of alcohol explained, in part, the man's belligerence.

Nate, stepping between them, said simply, "That's enough."

"Who the hell asked you to butt in?" the mule

skinner jeered. His clothes, his very body, reeked worse than the alcohol, and when he showed his teeth in a snarl, they were yellow, not white. He was big, almost as big as Nate, with an unkempt beard in dire need of a washing and a jagged scar down his left cheek. "I should pound you into the ground, you son of a bitch."

Nate casually handed his Hawken rifle to St. Vrain, casually turned, and casually hit the mule skinner a solid punch to the gut that doubled him over and turned the man's face near-purple. "That's enough out of you."

"Watch out!" Ceran St. Vrain cried.

The other two mule skinners were rushing to help their friend. They were not as big, but they were whipcord and vinegar, and never hesitated. Together they hurled themselves at Nate, one attacking high, the other diving low.

Leaping into the air, Nate avoided the tackle even as his right fist lashed out and connected with a gristly chin. His feet came down hard on the one who had tried to tackle him, eliciting a yelp of pain. Skipping sideways, Nate set himself just as the big mule skinner who had shoved St. Vrain came at him with both knobby fists swinging.

Nate blocked, dodged, struck. He was not without experience at rough and tumble, which he proved by landing several swift flicks that set the big mule skinner back on his heels.

The three were filthy and they stunk, but they were not stupid. They separated to come at Nate from different directions. One was bleeding from the mouth and another had his arm pressed to his side.

"Whoever you are, mister," said the mule skinner who had started it all, "we're about to whittle you down to size." His hand came from behind his back holding a doubled-edged knife with an antler handle.

"You don't want to do that," Nate said.

"Sure I do."

The mule skinner feinted at Nate's groin, then thrust at his throat. Nate, expecting the man to fight as dirty as he looked, twisted aside. The blade missed, but not by much. As quick as a thought, Nate grabbed the man's outstretched arm, gripping it by the wrist and the elbow, and brought his knee up. There was a distinct *crack* and the man howled like a stricken wolf and staggered back, the knife falling from fingers gone limp.

"Damn your hide!" one of the others roared as he and the third man closed in.

Nate unleashed an uppercut that started at his knee and ended somewhere above the clouds. It lifted the second mule skinner off the ground and stretched him out like a board.

That left the last, who suddenly lost interest. Holding his hands up, palms out, he said, "Enough, mister. We know when we're licked."

Nate had half a mind to knock him down anyway. But by then half a dozen of St. Vrain's staff had rushed to the aid of their employer.

The mule skinners were seized, none too gently, and escorted—one might say dragged—into the blacksmith shop.

"I am sorry about this," St. Vrain said, handing the Hawken back. "The rowdier element usually has enough sense not to cause trouble. They know I won't tolerate it."

"What will you do with them?" Nate asked. Not that he gave a good damn. He would as soon drop them headfirst from the ramparts.

"The one who pulled a knife on you will be banned from the fort for life," St. Vrain said. "The other two will be fined. If they refuse to pay, they too will be banned." He made for the blacksmith's.

The majority of freight outfits bound to and from Santa Fe laid over at Bent's Fort to load or un-load and take on provisions. Mule skinners banned from the post were of no use to their em-ployers. Consequently, the concerns that hired them often let them go.

The delay chafed at Nate's nerves. He was anx-ious to learn the fate of the presents he had ordered from a firm in Pennsylvania that specialized in fine china. As he stood there debating whether to go into the blacksmith shop, a hand fell lightly on his shoulder.

"Mr. King?"

Nate turned. It was Allan Decker, the head clerk. "Tell me you found them," Nate hopefully prodded.

"Yes and no." Decker's crestfallen expression hinted the news would not be to Nate's liking. "I have a general idea where the washbasin and the pitcher are."

"A general idea?" Nate repeated.

"Yes, sir." Decker fidgeted and would not meet Nate's gaze. "I'm afraid a new employee made the mistake of selling them."

Nate rarely lost his temper. He came close now. "He what?"

Adam's apple bobbing, Decker said, "A new clerk. He overheard a young woman mention to her husband how she would like a pitcher and he remembered seeing the fancy one in the back room. He had no idea it was yours, Mr. King. No idea it was being held for you. No one told him."

"So he sold it to her."

"The pitcher and the washbasin both, yes. About eight days ago. I'm awfully sorry. Mr. St. Vrain will be extremely upset."

"He's not the only one." Nate let out a sigh. So much for surprising Winona. "By now the pitcher and the basin must be halfway to Santa Fe."

"No, sir," Decker said.

Hope flared anew. Nate impulsively gripped the clerk by the shoulders. "The young couple are still here at the post?"

"I'm afraid not, sir. But neither were they bound for Santa Fe."

Nate thought he understood. "They were on

their way east instead of west? To St. Louis, maybe?"

"No, sir. They told the new man that they were on their way south."

Puzzlement furrowed Nate's brow. "But there's nothing to the south but grass, buffalo, and hostiles."

"You know that and I know that, Mr. King. But the young couple apparently got it into their heads that they were going to start up a farm."

"Dear God." Nate had heard some harebrained notions in his time, but this one bordered on insane. "Did the clerk happen to catch the handles of these two simpletons?"

"That he did, sir. The couple who have your pitcher and washbasin go by the names of Shipley and Cynthia Beecher."

CHAPTER TWO

The young couple on horseback had been riding for days. Both horses were sorrels. Both were more used to pulling plows than having saddles cinched to their backs.

The man was of less than average height. He had milky blue eyes and no chin to speak of. He was rail thin except for his shoulders. Farm work had molded them into bundles of muscles. He wore homespun and boots and a hat with a floppy brim that did little to keep the sun from his eyes. Strapped to his waist was a knife, but it was behind his left hip, where it would be difficult to reach quickly if the need arose. Slung across his back by a cord was a rifle. He rode slouched forward, his arms constantly flapping.

The woman was well under average height. Everything about her was small: small nose, small mouth, small ears, small fingers. She looked delicate, even fragile, but the manner in which she held herself hinted she was tougher than was apparent. Her eyes, too, were blue, but hers were piercing and bright. She wore a dress she had made herself, as she had made the man's shirt and pants. Where his hair was sandy, hers was as yellow as the fiery orb that dominated the sky.

Strangely, it was the woman who led their packhorse. Strange, too, was the fact she rode with much more assurance than the man, and with a lot less flopping about.

Beside the woman's horse, not the man's, loped a dog. The dog, too, was small, more mongrel than anything else. A dusky brown, the dog had a high forehead and a long muzzle. When, from time to time, the dog glanced up at the woman, unmistakable affection lit its dark eyes. No such affection was apparent when it glanced at the man.

The new day was only an hour old, yet already it was unbearably hot. The woman kept looking behind her, and finally, after the tenth or eleventh time, called out, "Rein up, Ship."

The man did so. He gazed quizzically at her as she came to a stop next to him. "What is it, Cyn?" He always called her that. Not Cynthia, but Cyn. Just as she always called him Ship instead of Shipley, but at his request since he liked Ship better.

"I am sure we are being followed."

"You claimed the same thing yesterday, and the

day before." Shipley Beecher frowned and stared in the direction they had come. "I still don't see anyone."

"There is someone back there, I tell you," Cynthia said. "Whoever it is has been following us for some time, but they never show themselves."

"To what end?" Ship responded. "If they were whites out to waylay us, surely they would have done so by now. If it were hostiles, surely they would have attacked before this." He smiled tolerantly and tolerantly shook his head. "No, I am afraid that female nature of yours is letting this get to you."

"Quit that," Cynthia said sharply.

"Quit what?"

"That talk about my female nature. You do it all the time, as if my being female makes me flighty and weak. I am neither and you well know it."

Ship leaned forward. "Are you going to start again? I swear, I can't say a thing to you some days without you taking exception."

"If you don't want me to take exception, don't say silly things about females," Cynthia said resentfully.

"But you *are* female, and you can't help being as females are," Ship said. "You fret over trifles and make mountains out of anthills."

Cynthia's blue eyes flashed. "I hate it when you do that. I just hate it."

"And I refuse to get into another argument over something so silly." Ship rose in the stirrups and stared for over a minute along their back trail, then sank back down. "Still no one. Not a speck."

"Someone is stalking us. I feel it in my bones."

"Ah," Ship said. "Your bones. Well, then, there can't be any mistake, can there? I mean, your bones never lie."

"Sarcasm ill becomes you."

"You want me to be serious? Fine, I'll be serious. How can you pester me with trifles when I have so much on my mind? My brothers are out here somewhere, and I intend to find them if it takes until winter."

The resentment on Cynthia's face softened. "It's been so long, Ship. They would have sent a letter."

"Don't talk like that. They are alive. They found a likely spot for our farms and have been too busy to get word to us."

Cynthia opened her small mouth but closed it again. She looked off across the sea of grass; then at the dog, which wagged its tail; then at her husband. "That must be it, Ship."

Shipley Beecher did not appear to notice her lack of conviction. "Of course it is. We'll come across them any day now."

The dog suddenly turned to the west and growled.

"What's the matter with Byron?"

"He must smell or hear something," Cynthia said. The dog was more hers than his. She had found it when it was but a puppy, lost and alone and skin and bones, wandering the streets of South Bend. She had brought it back to their farm and named it after her favorite poet. "Maybe it's whoever is following us."

"In which case they would be to the north, not the west," Ship noted. "No, that silly mutt of yours probably caught the scent of a rabbit or deer."

"He wouldn't growl without reason."

"There you go again. He's a dog, Cyn. He doesn't need a reason."

"Let's ride," Cynthia said. "Let's just ride."

That is what they did, until the sun was overhead and they and their mounts were caked with sweat. Cynthia, not Shipley, spotted the unusual sight up ahead, an oasis of vegetation covering more than an acre, and called out, "What's that?"

Ship stirred and straightened. "Trees, by God! It's a stand of trees! There must be water! It's the first we've come across since leaving the Platte. None too soon, either. Our water skins are about dry."

"How did those trees get there?" Cynthia wondered. It was her understanding that they did not sprout out of thin air.

"Who knows? Who cares?" Ship laughed. "Water, by God! I might have to dig for it but it's there."

No digging was required. A spring lay serene in the shade of overspreading boughs.

"I told you!" Ship declared, and started to swing down.

That was when the undergrowth on the other side parted and out stepped a man leading a horse. "How do you do, folks? Yes, indeed, how do you do?"

Shipley froze in surprise. Cynthia instantly leveled her rifle and said, "Stay, Byron! Stay!" The dog bared its teeth and crouched.

Old, greasy buckskins clung to the man's rangy form. The black hair that spilled from under his hat gave the impression of being coated with bear fat. His right eye was brown and kept twitching. Where his left eye should have been was a buckskin patch, tied fast. He had a bony face and a long nose and a slit of a mouth. He was armed with pistols and a rifle, but he held the rifle out from his side, barrel up. "I don't mean no harm, folks. I truly do not."

"What do you want?"

"Well, now, little lady, it's like this. I was fixing to wet my throat when I heard you folks coming and hid in case you were redskins."

"You haven't been following us, have you?" Cynthia asked suspiciously.

"How could I be doing that, little lady, when I am heading south, the same as you, and I reached this spring first, which means I was in front of you?"

"You could have passed us," Cynthia said.

"What is this, little lady?" the man said. "Can't a coon be neighborly?"

Ship finally spoke. "Cyn, quit pointing that rifle at him." Dismounting, he walked over, offered his hand, and introduced them.

"They call me One-Eye. One-Eye Jackson." The man in the greasy buckskins tapped the patch. "Never guess why."

Grinning, Ship said, "You must forgive my wife. You know how high-strung women can be."

"That I do," One-Eye said. He smiled at Cynthia, but she did not repay the courtesy. Shrugging, he turned to Shipley. "If you don't mind my asking, what in blazes are you two doing out here? Don't you know this is Injun country? Hostiles are everywhere."

"We haven't seen sign of any," Ship said.

"You never do, sonny, until it's too late." One-Eye gazed about the stand. "Injuns come to this spring all the time. I figured to slip in, fill my water skin, and slip out again. You'd be wise to do the same."

Cynthia had stayed where she was. "If you're so afraid of Indians," she now said, "what are *you* doing here?"

"Eh?" One-Eye's one eye blinked. "Tarnation. You're sure not a trusting she-cat, are you?"

"You haven't answered the question."

"If you must know," One-Eye said, "I'm after buffalo. Maybe you've heard of them. Big hairy critters with horns."

Cynthia's tone acquired an icy tinge. "I am well aware of what buffalo are. I am also aware of what polecats are. Which is why I consider it peculiar that you are out here in Injun country, as you so quaintly call it, hunting buffalo all by your lonesome."

"Little lady," One-Eye said, "the whole blamed West is Injun country. Up near Canada it's the Blackfeet. Lower down it's the Sioux. There are the Cheyenne, the Arapahos, the Utes, the Shoshones, the Bannocks, the Nez Perce. South of here are the Kiowas, the Comanches, the Apaches."

"You certainly know your Indians," Cynthia said. "Is your acquaintance with the truth as broad-reaching?"

"What does that mean?" One-Eye asked. "Are you saying I'm some kind of liar?"

Cynthia smiled sweetly. "There are blackbirds and there are doves, and you do not strike me as a dove."

One-Eye swung toward Shipley. "Pardon my language, mister, but what in hell does this contrary filly of yours have against me?"

"That's enough, Cyn," Ship said wearily. "We should be thankful he's white and not after our scalp."

"There are whites and there are whites," Cynthia said.

"There she goes again," One-Eye complained. "If she isn't addlepated, no one is."

Ship smiled and changed the subject. "My throat is parched and that water looks delicious." Sinking onto a knee, he cupped his left hand and dipped it in the spring. "Nice and cool, too." He sipped from his palm. "You should try some, Cyn. It's about the best water I've ever tasted."

"Sure is," One-Eye heartily agreed. "And the only water for miles around. Which is why you shouldn't dawdle. Every tribe from here to creation knows about this spring."

"I don't notice you drinking," Cynthia observed. "Yet you said you were thirsty."

"Enough, Cyn," Ship said. "Must you carp so? Let's do as he suggests. Fill our water skins and leave before we're discovered."

"I doubt there is anyone else within fifty miles," Cynthia said, but under her breath so the rangy frontiersman would not hear. Dismounting, she stepped to the packhorse and loudly asked, "Do I do all the work or will you help me?"

Shipley hurried to her side. "Need you ask?" Out of the corner of his mouth he whispered, "Must you behave so? Would it hurt to be polite?"

"I don't trust him."

"You never trust anyone. Heck, when we first met, you didn't trust me." Ship untied the two water skins and gave the one that was almost empty to her. "You didn't trust my brothers, either, yet Hiram and Elmer became two of your very best friends."

"I wish they were here now," Cynthia said. "I

wish they never went off on their gallivant. I was content in Indiana."

One-Eye was watching them intently. "Is something wrong? What's all the whispering about?"

"Married talk," Cynthia answered.

"Cyn, please," Shipley said. Squatting, he opened the water skin and plunged the neck under the surface. Bubbles erupted, and he lowered the entire skin.

"Is it me," One-Eye said, "or do you two bicker a lot?"

"Suppose you tell us a little about yourself," Ship said, "and don't worry about my wife and me?"

One-Eye's grin twisted his scar. "Sure, sonny, sure. Don't twist your britches in a knot." He smiled at Cynthia, but she might as well have been carved from granite. "There's not much to tell, though. I came west in '40. Heard a heap about the trapping trade and figured I would be rolling in money. Made it to the rendezvous along the Green River. Only thing was, the bottom had fallen out of the beaver market, and that was the last rendezvous ever held."

"An uncle told me about them," Shipley said. "I would dearly have loved to attend one. According to him they were quite colorful."

"Sonny, you don't know the half of it," One-Eye assured him. "The caravan had pretty near thirty carts and about forty men. Not counting the wagons of the emigrants and the missionaries." He placed the stock of his rifle on the ground and leaned on the muzzle. "Jim Bridger guided us, and Joel Walker, the brother of Joe Walker, was also along."

"I would like to meet Bridger," Shipley said.

"He's a hoot. You'd never guess how famous he is to meet him in person. He's up there with the likes of Joe Walker, Kit Carson, Joe Meek, and Nate King." One-Eye spoke the last name with a spiteful rasp.

"My uncle told me that a lot of Indians attended the rendezvous."

"Did they ever!" One-Eye exclaimed. "Why, when we got to the Green River, hundreds of Snakes came to meet us. Shoshones, some call them. Must've been every blamed warrior in the tribe, wearing what they take for finery. You never saw so many wolves' tails, bear teeth, and cougar claws. They favored feathers, too, and pearls, those who could get them in trade. Such a hullabaloo! They rode around the camp three times, whooping and shouting and waving their coup sticks with scalps tied at the ends—"

Shipley glanced pointedly at Cynthia. "Maybe you shouldn't talk about scalps and such in front of my wife."

"Is she squeamish?" One-Eye asked, and tittered.

"No," Cynthia said. "And neither do I suffer fools with much patience. You would do well to keep that in mind."

One-Eye did not take offense. "You're a feisty wench, I'll say that for you. But back to the rendezvous. Some Flatheads showed up. So did a few Crows. But it was mostly the damned Snakes."

"Wait a minute," Ship said. "A man at Bent's Fort claimed that the Snakes or Shoshones or whatever you call them are the friendliest tribe anywhere."

"So folks say," One-Eye sourly replied. "But you couldn't prove it by me." He tapped his eye patch. "Or by this."

"The Shoshones did that to you?"

One-Eye nodded. "That they did, sonny. Pried my eyeball right out with the tip of a knife."

Cynthia stepped to the spring to dip her water skin. "What did you do to deserve it?"

"Cyn!" Ship said.

"That's all right," One-Eye said. "I expect that of your filly. For her information, I didn't do anything. But those devils didn't need a reason. A bunch of Snakes held me down and a buck named Touch The Clouds dug my eye out."

"That doesn't sound like something the Shoshones would do," Cynthia said.

Shipley was more sympathetic. "How horrible."

"It was worse than horrible," One-Eye said, and shuddered. "I can remember the feel of the steel as it slid under my eye. I can remember the pain."

"We don't need to hear more."

"I couldn't lift a finger. They had me flat on my back. I howled and I cussed and I begged, but it didn't do a lick of good. They held me, and the coyote with the knife did the deed." One-Eye touched his hand to the patch. "Want to see the hole?"

"Good Lord, no!" Ship replied. "Are you insane? There is a lady present."

One-Eye rubbed the patch, then traced his scar with a fingertip. "They did this that night, too, the filthy heathens. Ever since, I've hated the Snakes and anyone who has anything to do with them."

"I don't blame you," Shipley said. "Not if they did it unjustly."

"I said that was how it was, didn't I?" One-Eye snapped. "Or are you starting to act like your wife?"

"Now, see here," Ship objected. "You will stop speaking ill of the woman I love. I will tolerate a lot but not that."

The frontiersman's slit of a mouth curled in a lopsided grin. "Whatever you want, sonny. I reckon I don't hold my tongue like I should. That comes from spending so much time alone. I forget how to act around folk like yourselves."

"I doubt that very much," Cynthia said. "You're a shrewd coyote, is what you are. That tale of yours doesn't earn a tear from me."

"You're something, little lady," One-Eye replied. "Yes, indeed. As tart a tongue as I've ever come across." He turned away from the spring and snagged the reins to his mount. "You don't need to beat me with a war club. I know when my company isn't wanted." One-Eye placed his hands on his saddle. Suddenly he pointed. "I'll be damned. I warned you, didn't I, but you wouldn't listen."

Shipley and Cynthia rose, leaving the water skins, and peered through the cottonwoods to the southeast.

"What are you talking about?" Ship asked. "There's nothing there."

"You don't see the dust?"

"What dust?" Cynthia demanded. "The sky is as clear as clear can be."

One-Eye jabbed at the horizon. "There's dust, I tell you. Injuns. Heading for this spring."

Ship moved past him to see better. "Dust is dust. It could be a herd of buffalo or wild horses."

"It could be antelope, too, or prairie dogs having a frolic." One-Eye snickered. "But it's not any of them. I lied."

"You what?"

"Lied about a lot of it except for the rendezvous and my eye. But I had to trick you until you were where I wanted you and now you are."

Shipley began to turn. "You're not making any sen—"

One-Eye Jackson swept the heavy hardwood stock of his rifle up and around in a tight arc. His was a Kentucky rifle, an older model reliable at long distances. The butt of the stock was reinforced with a metal plate, and it was the metal

plate that smashed into Shipley Beecher's temple
with enough force to nearly split Shipley's skull.
He folded without a sound or a twitch.

For precious seconds Cynthia was rooted in
shock. Then One-Eye Jackson looked at her, and
leered, and the spell was broken. "Sic him, Byron!" she yelled. "Sic him, boy!"

The mongrel came up off its haunches in a blur.
Two bounds, and Byron cleared the spring, jaws
spread wide to rend.

It seemed to Cynthia that Jackson was as good
as ripped to shreds. But she had forgotten that he
had spent years in the wilds, that he was a frontiersman, and that frontiersmen, both the good
ones and the bad ones, lived on the razor's edge
of their reflexes every waking moment of their
lives. She thought Jackson would be ripped to
shreds but she was wrong.

One-Eye spun more swiftly than a human being should be able to spin, and the same stock
that brought Shipley low slammed into Byron's
high forehead. The dog yipped once and fell mo-
tionless at One-Eye's feet.

"So much for your protectors."

Fleeting fear caused Cynthia to back away.
Then reason asserted itself, reason and a red-hot
wave of anger that filled her veins with molten
fire. "You miserable vermin," she said, and immediately brought her rifle to bear. Hers was a
short-barreled rifle made by N. Kiles of Raccoon

Creek, Ohio. Only .33 caliber, it was adequate for a man but not anything bigger.

One-Eye sprang as Cynthia squeezed the trigger. She thought she had him. She thought the ball would core his belly and leave him helpless and near death. But there was no blast, no explosion of smoke and lead. She had not thumbed the hammer back. Instantly, Cynthia sought to remedy her blunder, but Jackson was on her before she could. With a savage wrench, he tore the rifle from her grasp and hurled it a good ten feet.

"Try to shoot me, will you?"

Few times in her life had Cynthia ever been struck. Her mother had slapped her on occasion when she was small, but that was it. Shipley never hit her. He was not the type. So the blow to her cheek was doubly enervating.

"That's just for starters," One-Eye Jackson said.

Cynthia had lost her rifle, but she still had a flintlock pistol tucked at her waist. Frantic, she clawed at it, her fingers wrapping tight. She barely had it clear of her belt when hideous pain and blinding light burst in her head. The world shimmered and shook. She was vaguely aware of falling. A veil of darkness descended but only for a moment or two. Then her vision cleared and she was staring up into the scarred visage of the monster who had laid her low. She got her elbows under her and attempted to rise.

"No, you don't."

Iron fingers clamped onto Cynthia's throat, choking off her breath. She pried at the fingers but could not loosen them.

"That's it," One-Eye said. "Fight me. I like it when they put up a struggle. Especially the pretty ones, like you." His laugh was gleefully vicious.

Cynthia struggled harder. She tried to rake his good eye with her fingernails, but he jerked back, cackling.

"You were right, little lady," One-Eye crowed. "I *was* following you. I shadowed you and your weak sister of a husband all the way from Bent's Fort." With his other hand he caressed her hair. "I don't need to tell you why, do I?"

Cynthia attempted to knee him where it would hurt a man the most, but he twisted his hip, deflecting her knee.

One-Eye licked his lips. "Think of yourself as a bowl of pudding, and me, I have a sweet tooth."

CHAPTER THREE

Stark terror welled in Cynthia Beecher, but she fought it down. She was a scrapper, as her grandmother used to say. When she was a child she was often picked on for her small size, and she learned early in life to stand up for herself. Later, but before she met Shipley, she had to ward off the advances of men who seemed to think that being bigger gave them the natural right to let their hands roam where they wanted. She proved them wrong.

But Cynthia had never been in a situation like this. Never had her virtue, and her life, been in imminent peril.

One-Eye Jackson put his other hand on her bosom. "I think I'll rip your dress off and take it from there."

Cynthia could count the number of times she

had used swear words in her life on one hand. She swore now. "Bastard!" She clawed at his face, but he swatted her arm aside.

"You'll have to do better than that, little lady," One-Eye mocked, then slugged her in the stomach.

Again, Cynthia's world swam. She almost cried out, almost gave him the satisfaction of hearing her bleat in fear. Inexplicably, the pressure on her throat eased, as did the weight of Jackson's legs on hers. Wildly, blindly, she scrambled backward, but he did not pounce. Suddenly the world stopped spinning and she could see again. The only thing was, what she saw mystified her.

One-Eye Jackson was suspended in midair. He appeared to be floating a couple of feet off the ground. His head was bent at an angle, and he was thrashing his arms and legs.

Bewildered, Cynthia sat up. It was then she saw the man behind Jackson. It was another frontiersman in buckskins. Only this one had a powerful chest and broad shoulders and stood well over six feet.

"Who—" One-Eye squawked. "What—"

Belatedly, Cynthia saw that the other frontiersman had Jackson by the back of the neck and was holding him in the air by sheer strength of sinew, a feat so marvelous she would not credit it as possible were she not witnessing it with her own eyes.

"You owe the lady an apology," the newcomer said in a deep, rumbling voice. His green eyes darted to her. "Are you all right?"

"Yes," Cynthia found herself saying. The only thing hurt was her dignity. Shipley was the one in need of attention.

The giant reached around and stripped Jackson of his flintlocks and knife and tossed them to one side. As if Jackson weighed no more than a feather, the giant flung him to the ground. One-Eye instantly sought to rise and received a kick in the ribs. "Stay where you are."

One-Eye looked up. His sweat-streaked face paled. "You!"

"Me," the man said. To his rear, propped against a cottonwood, was a Hawken rifle. "You should check on your husband," he said to Cynthia. Drawing a pistol, he cocked it and trained it on Jackson. "Need I warn you that one wrong move and you will be worm food?"

"What are you doing here?" One-Eye demanded. "You, of all people!"

Cynthia rushed to Shipley. He did not stir when she touched him. On his temple was a knot the size of a hen's egg. Blood trickled from a gash. She felt his wrist and detected a strong but slow pulse. "He's alive, thank God!"

"Wet a cloth," her rescuer said.

Cynthia dashed to the packhorse. In one of the packs was a washcloth. She hastily soaked it in the spring, then cradled Shipley's head in her lap and gently dabbed at the hen's egg. "Thank heaven you came along when you did, whoever you are."

* * *

"Nate King," Nate introduced himself, not taking his eyes off Jackson. "And I'm not here by chance." He did not tell her about the pitcher. Or about nearly riding the bay into the ground to overtake them before they encountered hostiles.

"Oh?" Cynthia was too worried about Shipley for the comment to fully sink in. "That awful man would have murdered us if you hadn't come."

"He's killed before," Nate said.

One-Eye Jackson rolled onto his back. "I heard tell you moved way off in the mountains."

"I was out for a stroll."

"Like hell." One-Eye's remaining eye blazed with hate. "You were tracking me, weren't you? You've wanted me dead for years and finally got around to tracking me down."

"I wouldn't soil my hands," Nate said. "But the Shoshones would like to get theirs on you."

Fear replaced One-Eye's hate. "You wouldn't!" he gasped. "You know what they would do to me! You can't let them do that to a white man."

"Why can't I?" Nate responded. "It would be fitting."

Cynthia had folded the cloth into a compress and applied it to her husband's brow. "What are you two talking about?"

"The Shoshones have an old score to settle with Mr. Jackson, here," Nate informed her, but he did not elaborate.

"He told us they were the ones who cut out his eye," Cynthia said.

"They would have carved him into tiny pieces, but he got away."

Cynthia raised her head. "Wait a minute. He mentioned you, too. Something about you being as well known as Kit Carson."

"Kit is probably the most famous scout alive," Nate said. "Compared to him, I'm small potatoes."

One-Eye licked his thin lips. "What do you intend to do with me, King? Are you really going to turn me over to the Snakes?"

"I should."

Shipley Beecher picked that moment to groan. His eyelids fluttered and an arm moved.

"Be still, dearest," Cynthia urged. She ran her fingers through his sandy hair, careful not to brush the hen's egg.

Unwilling to let the matter of his fate drop, One-Eye said to Nate, "I want to know, damn you! Are you fixing to hand me over to your red kin?"

Nate ignored the question. Tilting his head back, he uttered a piercing whistle. Cynthia Beecher looked at him quizzically and received her answer when the undergrowth crackled and through the trees came Nate's bay. Sweat lathered its chest, and it was covered with the dust of many miles. Bobbing its head, the bay came to Nate and nuzzled him.

"You've trained your horse well."

"He's an old friend," Nate said with affection. He patted the bay's neck, then opened a parfleche decorated with blue beads—Winona's handiwork—and took out a coil of rope. To Jackson he said, "Sit up with your hands behind your back."

"Like hell I will," the cyclops growled.

"Like hell you won't," Nate retorted, and extended his pistol.

One-Eye swore. "You would do it, too. You always have loved Injuns more than your own kind."

Nate warily sidled around behind him, saying, "You lived with a Shoshone woman once."

"Don't remind me. Taking up with her was the worst mistake of my life. It cost me an eye."

"No, *you* cost yourself the eye," Nate said. "There are some things a man just doesn't do. Not ever."

"Who are you to judge?" One-Eye snapped. "I'll never forget what you did. Never forget how you wouldn't stand up for me."

Cynthia glanced from one to the other. "I repeat. What are you two talking about? What happened, Mr. King, that this horrible man hates you so?"

Again Nate ignored the question. Instead, he squatted and pressed the muzzle to the nape of Jackson's neck. "Give me an excuse. Any excuse." Placing the flintlock on the ground, he grasped the rope in both hands and went to loop it around Jackson's wrists.

The instant the rope touched his skin, Jackson erupted in lightning motion. Slamming his shoulder against Nate's to unbalance him, Jackson bolted like a rabbit and was in among the trees in the blink of an eye.

"He's getting away!" Cynthia cried.

Nate scooped up his flintlock and took a quick bead, but he could not get a clear shot for all the cottonwoods. Surging to his feet, he gave chase. He did not think to grab the Hawken. Plunging headlong through the undergrowth, he covered twenty yards without spotting his quarry. One-Eye, Nate suspected, had sought cover. Stopping in midstride, he crouched and probed the stand with his every sense alert. He heard nothing, saw nothing.

"Mr. King?"

Nate hoped the woman would have the good sense not to yell anything else. Jackson was no *mangeur de lard*, no greener. When Jackson needed to, he could move like a wraith. Nate bided his time, hoping Jackson would give away his location, but the stand was conspicuous by its silence.

"Mr. King? Are you all right?"

Reluctantly, Nate returned to the spring. He crammed the rope back in the parfleche, reclaimed his Hawken, retrieved the weapons he had taken from One-Eye, and put the pistols and knife in a different parfleche. One-Eye's rifle he lashed on the Beechers' pack animal.

Cynthia was moistening the cloth when Nate hunkered beside her. "Shouldn't Ship have come out of it by now?"

"There's no predicting head wounds." Nate examined it. The flesh wasn't discolored, which was a good sign. "I have something that will help him when he revives."

"I want to thank you, again, for coming to our aid. That terrible man said he had followed us all the way from Bent's Fort."

"He did," Nate confirmed. "His tracks overlaid yours. I didn't know who it was. But I figured it didn't bode well."

"You haven't told me why you two despise each other so much."

"Some things are better left unsaid," Nate replied. To divert her curiosity, he examined the dog, which was stirring, and asked, "What in God's name are you doing here, anyway?"

"We needed water. What else? We had no idea he was waiting here for us. I distrusted him the moment I laid eyes on him. Unfortunately, my husband gave him the benefit of the doubt."

"Too much trust can get you killed," Nate said. "But I didn't mean *here*." He pointed at the spring. "I meant *here*." And he encompassed the prairie with a sweep of his arm.

"Oh. We aim to have us a farm. Ship and his brothers and their families and me. A year from now we'll be snug in our sod houses and have crops we can sell for cash money."

"If you're still alive." Nate sat back and asked while scouring the vegetation for Jackson, "Do you have any idea where you are?"

"What a strange thing to ask," Cynthia said. "We're somewhere between Bent's Fort and Texas."

"Do you know what this part of the prairie is called?"

"I wouldn't have the foggiest."

"Comanche Grass. The Comanches live to the south, but hunting and war parties stray up this way every once in a while. Most folks won't go anywhere near here because they know they would never come out again."

"The only Indians we've seen were the tame ones at the trading post," Cynthia said.

"Comanches are anything but tame," Nate assured her. "If they catch you in their territory, they will do things to you I could not begin to describe to a lady. As soon as your husband is up and about, I'm taking you to Bent's Fort."

"He will refuse to go."

"No farm is worth your lives."

"It's not that. It's his brothers. They came out ahead of us to find a suitable spot for our farms. They reached Bent's Fort and sent a letter back with a wagon train saying how they were ready to strike off across the prairie. That was the last anyone heard from them."

"It will be the last anyone hears from you if you don't persuade your husband to give up the search." Nate thought he heard a soft sound to his rear and pivoted on the balls of his feet.

"What is it?" Cynthia nervously asked.

"Apparently nothing." Nate straightened and held his Hawken ready for swift use. Jackson was undoubtedly watching them; he would not go far, not without his weapons and his horse. Nate scanned the plain, not really expecting to see anything, but then he stiffened.

Cynthia slid her legs out from under her husband. "What did you do that for?" she asked as she stood. "And don't tell me it's nothing."

"Dust. To the south."

Her eyes narrowing, Cynthia took a step. "Jackson said the same thing, but I didn't see any dust then and I don't see any dust now."

"It's there." Years of living in the wilderness had honed Nate's senses to an exceptional degree. His ears, his nose, his eyes were sharper than the dull organs of those who lived east of the Mississippi. Those who never had to fret about taking an arrow or a slug, or being torn asunder by the slavering jaws and blood-tipped claws of some savage beast.

"That wretched man said it might be Indians."

"More likely it's a herd of buffalo, grazing," Nate guessed. Once each year the buffalo migrated from north to south and back again. The rest of the time, they roamed widely, seeking fresh grass to fill their bellies.

"Then it's not any of those Comanches you are so worried about?"

"Let's hope not." Nate would be hard pressed to save his own hide. Saving theirs might be impossible. The Comanches were fierce warriors. Some folks would say they were *the* most fierce. As formidable as Apaches, if not more so.

At that juncture Shipley Beecher groaned and slowly sat up. Wincing, he pressed his hand to the bird's egg. "I have the grandmother of all headaches." He smiled at Cynthia, and gave a start. "The rap on my noggin must be worse than I thought. Either the vermin who hit me has tripled in size or you went and swapped him for a giant."

Dropping onto a knee, Cynthia tenderly clasped his hand in hers. "He's a friend, Ship. His name is Nate King. He saved me from the other one."

Shipley grew red from the neck up. "Where is the Satan spawn? The Bible says an eye for an eye. I say a head for a head should make us even."

"One-Eye ran off," Cynthia revealed. "But we have his guns and his horse. We'll take them with us."

"And leave him afoot?"

Nate King was surprised by Beecher's reaction. "Jackson nearly killed you and tried to violate your wife. A few seconds ago you were fit to bury him. Now you're having second thoughts?"

"Giving him a taste of his own medicine is one thing," Ship said. "Stooping to his vile level is another."

"Dead is dead," Nate said.

"I don't agree. I might be a simple farmer, but I never do anything that goes against my upbringing." Shipley attempted to stand and had to stop when his legs wobbled like sticks in a high wind. "Tarnation. I'm weaker than I thought."

Cynthia appealed to Nate. "My husband needs rest and tending. Can we stay here the rest of the day? Or overnight perhaps?"

"We'll see," was the best answer Nate could give her. With Jackson lurking somewhere in the stand, it was not wise to stay any longer than was absolutely necessary. While she devoted herself to Shipley, Nate brought the horses closer to the spring and picketed them. By then the dog had recovered and was lying next to Cynthia. It growled at him and Cynthia hushed it.

Gathering firewood was an easy chore. There were plenty of fallen limbs. He broke the limbs into suitable lengths and stacked them in a pile.

In addition to the pair of pistols and the bowie knife and tomahawk Nate customarily wore around his waist, he had an ammo pouch and a possibles bag slanted crosswise across his broad chest. From the latter he now removed a fire steel and flint and his tinderbox. The tinder was part of an old bird's nest he had found some time ago. Pinching enough to suffice, he placed it on a flat spot. By striking the oval fire steel against the flint, he produced sparks that landed on the tinder and set tiny swirls of smoke to rising. Puffing lightly, he nurtured a tiny flame and added dead leaves to make the flame grow. Soon he had a small fire crackling.

Nate replaced the steel, flint, and tinderbox in his possibles bag. Of all his possessions, it could be argued, they were the most essential. Steel and flint were the two items every mountain man carried with him everywhere he went. Trappers had always carried extra steels and flints to trade with.

Before the coming of the white man, most tribes relied on a fire drill and fire plow to start fires. It consumed a lot of time and not inconsiderable effort, whereas with a fire steel and flint and good tinder, a fire could be started in no time at all. Indians were no different than white men and liked anything that made their lives easier. They gratefully accepted them. The best aspect, from the white point of view, was that steels and flints only cost a penny or two, so the whites could be generous in handing them out.

From a parfleche on the bay Nate now took a small buckskin pouch, his coffeepot, and his battered tin cup. He filled the pot at the spring and set it to boil. When the water was bubbling, he poured some into the cup. Then, loosening the drawstring on the pouch, he added about a spoonful of a fine brown powder. He stirred this with a stick and placed the cup aside to cool.

Cynthia had been watching with keen interest. "What is that you have there?" she inquired.

"An herb that will do wonders for your husband. As soon as it cools, I'll make a poultice." Nate drew the drawstring tight.

"Is that medicine a doctor gave you?"

"My wife gathered the roots and ground them. She is quite the healer."

"An Indian remedy?"

"They are as good as anything the white man has come up with, and in some cases, better."

"You don't say?"

She sounded slightly skeptical, so Nate elaborated. "Indians have cures for everything under the sun." He wagged the pouch. "This here is the root of a wildflower, a geranium, I guess whites would call it."

"What are some of the other cures?"

"For inflammation, the Shoshones use the root of the elderberry plant. For sores, they rely on honeysuckle roots. For bloated stomachs, they make a tea from peppermint leaves. For female trouble, it's wormwood."

"Female trouble?" Cynthia said, and blushed slightly. "Oh. They even have something for that?"

"You would be surprised," Nate answered. "The women are partial to a tea made from juniper berries that they say keeps them from having babies."

Cynthia put a hand to her throat. "They abort their babies?"

"Not after the fact, as it were. Before."

"Oh my." Cynthia did not try to hide her amazement.

"Clematis bark makes a fine shampoo. From fir trees they make a face cream. From flowers they make a red rouge for their cheeks. From sweet pine they concoct an oil to make their hair shiny. Meadow rue makes a fine perfume. Old sagebrush leaves, crushed into a powder, are dandy for the backsides of babies with diaper rashes."

"I had no idea," Cynthia admitted. The dog nuzzled her leg, seeking attention, and she rubbed it. "Good boy, Byron."

"Indians use plants and roots for everything," Nate said. "For dyes, for chewing gum, for tonics."

Shipley Beecher, who had been lying on his back with his eyes closed, opened them and turned his head toward Nate. "You almost make it sound as if they are superior to the white man in some respects. But that can hardly be. They are primitives, after all."

Nate's sympathy for the farmer dropped several notches. "You're a man of fixed opinions, I take it?"

"Regarding certain matters, yes."

"Indians, for instance?" Nate fished.

"I won't lie to you, Mr. King. I am not as fond of them as you are, and I certainly would never marry one."

"Ship!" Cynthia said.

"No insult intended, my dear. But I would be less than candid if I did not confess that I regard the red man as the savage he is. Look at all the atrocities they have committed. Look at all the whites they have killed. They are a hindrance to the spread of civilization."

"What you are saying," Nate said quietly, "is that you agree with the view that all Indians should be rounded up and herded onto reservations."

"Why deny it?" Shipley responded. "Their ways are not our ways. They have no place in the white world."

"They were here first," Nate noted. "This land is their land."

"Oh, please. I am not dumb. I know, for instance, that many tribes regard land as belonging to everyone. They have no notion of private property. I ask you, how ridiculous is that?"

Nate did not say anything.

"Again, I mean no disrespect, Mr. King. I have nothing against those, like you, who adopt red ways. If that is what you want to do, fine. It is your life, after all. But do not expect the rest of us to hold the red race in the high regard you do when they have done nothing to merit it."

"Oh, Ship," Cynthia said softly.

"Will you stop?" Ship replied. "Mr. King and I

are grown men. I am sure he will not hold it against me. Will you, Mr. King?"

"I can't help how another person thinks," Nate said.

"There. I told you." Ship grinned at his wife. "Enough about the heathens. My head is throbbing. How about that poultice?"

CHAPTER FOUR

Twilight crept over the prairie like a thief stealing the day. Before darkness fell, Nate searched the stand from end to end. He poked into every thicket, examined every shadowy patch. But he found no trace of One-Eye Jackson.

On a hunch, Nate made a circuit of the edge of the stand. At a spot where the grass met the trees, south of the spring, he was rewarded for his diligence with a trail of flat blades. Something or some*one* had crawled off into the prairie grass.

Nate stayed in the stand. He suspected that Jackson was lying in wait for him out there, hoping to jump him if Nate went after him.

Cynthia busied herself cooking supper. The dog lay curled beside her. Among the victuals their packhorse was burdened with was cornmeal, yeast, and sugar, and she was in the process of making dodgers. She already had coffee perking, and had laid out salt pork and prepared succotash.

The aroma made Nate's mouth water. His own cooking was more than passable, but there was something about eating a meal cooked by another that made it doubly appealing. Hunkering, he filled his cup.

"Are we safe?" Shipley Beecher asked.

"As safe as anyone can be where nearly everyone and everything is out to kill you," Nate answered.

"Surely you exaggerate," Ship said. "It can't be as bad as all that or no one would live here. Not even the Indians."

Nate wondered why it was that so many people, white and red, judged others by their own standards. "This isn't like where you're from. Indiana, didn't your wife say?"

"Meaning what, exactly?" Ship asked with more than mild sarcasm.

"East of the Mississippi all the grizzlies have been killed off. A lot of the black bears, too. Cougars are rare in states where they were once plentiful. Wolves have pretty near been exterminated," Nate patiently detailed. "Every hostile tribe has been wiped out or forced to relocate."

"There are a few who still act up," Shipley remarked.

"But it's nothing like out here," Nate said. "In Indiana you can hike for miles through the deepest woods and all you will run into are squirrels and deer."

"I still say you exaggerate," Ship stubbornly insisted. "We never once set eyes on a hostile or even a griz the whole time we have been out here. Fact is, the most dangerous critter we came across was a coyote that ran off at the sight of us."

"You were lucky."

"Oh, please. Why can't you accept that the wilderness is not as danger-filled as you make it out to be?"

Cynthia broke her long silence. "He's concerned for our welfare, Ship. He knows this land better than we do."

"I must say, dear wife, that I am not at all sure why you keep sticking up for him. I'm your husband, after all. If you stick up for anyone it should be me. Not this fellow we hardly know."

"He saved our lives."

"So you keep pointing out," Ship said. "But I was not awake to see it, so you will have to forgive me if I am less than happy that he has attached himself to us."

Nate simmered inside. That was the last particle of insult he was willing to abide. Especially from someone who, in Nate's estimation, did not have a lick of common sense. "I will leave right this minute if you want."

"Whenever you're of a mind is fine by me," Shipley said.

"But not by me," Cynthia said. "How many times must I say the same thing? *He saved our lives.* He trailed us from Bent's Fort and arrived just in time."

Ship's whole body twitched. "Are you saying he followed us all the way from the trading post? To what end?"

"Shipley Beecher, you stop that."

"He wouldn't follow us so far unless he was after something of ours."

"He's not after anything!" Cynthia hotly declared.

"Actually," Nate said, "I am."

Shipley pushed to his feet. He did it too fast and swayed as if he were drunk, but it was a bout of dizziness from the blow to his head. "Aha! I knew it! He's out to rob us! What do you say about your buckskin-clad Lancelot now?"

"He is not anything to me except hopefully a friend," Cynthia said. She looked at Nate in mild bewilderment. "But why, in heaven's name? Our possessions don't amount to much, our clothes are plain, and our animals aren't much good except behind a plow."

"Steal us blind, that's what he aims to do!" Ship declared. "Take everything we own!"

"It's the pitcher and the washbasin," Nate said.

"The who?"

"The china pitcher and the china washbasin you bought at Bent's Fort," Nate clarified. "I ordered them special from back East and the clerk sold them to you by mistake."

"We owe our lives to a washbasin?" Shipley said, and laughed.

Cynthia appeared fit to cry. "And here I thought you saved us out of the goodness of your heart."

Ship was grinning from ear to ear. "He has destroyed my faith in human nature, and that's a fact."

"Cut it out, Ship,"Cynthia said. "You are not the least bit hilarious."

"From walking on water to as common as grass in the blink of an eye," Shipley said. "I believe that is some kind of record."

Nate let him prattle. "About the washbasin and the pitcher?"

"White with blue flowers," Cynthia said. "The finest china I ever set eyes on. I had no idea they were yours. No one told us."

"I would like to look at them," Nate said, indicating their pack animal. "I would like to look at them very much."

"You can't," Shipley Beecher said.

"I will pay you," Nate told him. "Pay you whatever you paid for them, and five dollars besides. They're for my wife. I bought them as a gift and dearly want to give them to her."

"Well, you still can't," Shipley said.

Nate tried counting to ten but it did not help. "Maybe I haven't made myself clear. They're mine.

I paid for them. They were sold to you by mistake, and I aim to have them whether you agree or don't agree."

Shipley gave his wife a smug look. "What do you think of your Lancelot now? Sort of tarnished, I'd say."

Nate slowly rose and began to open his possibles bag. "I have the money right here."

"You could pull out a poke filled with gold nuggets and you still can't have them." Shipley slapped his leg and snorted. "This is priceless. Isn't this priceless, dear?"

"Pay him no mind, Mr. King," Cynthia said. "He keeps saying you can't have them because we don't have them."

"How's that again? The clerk described the pair he sold the set to, and you two fit the bill."

"Oh, we bought the pitcher and the basin, all right, but I wasn't too keen on lugging them across the prairie and maybe having them break on me. So I left them at Bent's Fort."

"You what?" Nate was flabbergasted. No one at the post had mentioned any such thing.

"I left them with a man named William Bent," Cynthia explained. "He promised to hold them for me until we got back."

Suddenly Nate understood. Bent had not been at the fort when he was there. Ceran St. Vrain had mentioned that Bent was off visiting his wife's people, the Cheyenne. Odds were, Nate reflected, that Bent had left the pitcher and the washbasin in his office and not mentioned it to anyone, so St. Vrain had not thought to look there during the search.

Shipley Beecher could not stop laughing. "You came all this way for nothing! When I get home and tell this tale around the pickle barrel, my friends will split a gut."

Turning on his heel, Nate strode into the darkness. The farmer was grating on his nerves. Or was it something else? Preoccupied, he covered a dozen feet before he awakened to the mistake he was making. He stopped in midstride. The feeble glow cast by the fire did not penetrate very far. Blackness enveloped him. He could not see his hand at arm's length. And One-Eye might be anywhere. "Damn me for a dunce." Nate wheeled and started back.

The Beechers had not moved. They were still by the fire, but they were not looking at him. They were staring into the cottonwoods to the south, their expressions one of puzzlement. He was about to ask what was the matter when a loud grunt to his right supplied the answer. A huge form loomed, a vague bulk notable for its immense size and a distinct odor.

Byron growled and started forward, but Cynthia grabbed the dog by the scruff of its neck. "Stay, boy."

Stopping cold, Nate held himself perfectly still. He must not make a sound or move or he might not live out the night.

The creature lumbered off. Almost instantly another took its place, snorting noisily. A curved horn glinted, a natural scimitar that could disembowel man or beast with ease.

Shipley Beecher started to stand, but Cynthia grabbed his wrist and pulled him back down.

"Someone should shoo them off," Shipley objected.

"No," Cynthia said. "We don't know what they will do."

Nate did. He edged toward the fire, sliding first one foot and then the other. The colossus beside him faded into the gloom, emboldening him to run the rest of the way. Shipley was again trying to rise, but Cynthia would not let him.

"Sit back down!" Nate commanded. "It won't take much to provoke them."

"What are they doing here?" Cynthia whispered, apprehensive.

"They're thirsty," Nate answered. "But the fire and our scent are keeping them away." He added, "For now."

No sooner were the words out of his mouth than a gargantuan apparition hove out of the trees. It made no more noise than the sigh of the breeze. Advancing to within a lance-length of the spring, it regarded them with baleful malevolence.

The buffalo was enormous. Six feet high at the front shoulders, it had to weigh close to a ton. From nose to tail tip was at least ten feet. The horns had a three-foot spread. The brute was a nigh indestructible engine of destruction, a mountain of muscle that could hold its own against any creature in creation.

Abruptly, it whirled, and the spell was broken. On both sides of them passed a seemingly endless stream of shaggy behemoths.

Cynthia's eyes met Nate's. She was scared. It showed in her gaze, in her posture. But she did not give in to it. She did not scream, as many would have done, or jump up and bolt. She had the presence of mind to appreciate the consequences, and the self-control to stay put.

Shipley was another matter. Despite his wife's restraining grip on his wrist, he kept trying to rise. What he hoped to accomplish, Nate couldn't begin to guess. The huge, lumbering forms, their grunts and snorts, the odor and the dust they raised, should have been enough to convince Shipley there were too many buffalo for him to do anything about, but he would not stay down.

Nate gouged his Hawken into the farmer's side. He would never shoot, but Beecher did not know that. "Be still, damn you, or you'll get us killed."

"What about our horses? They might run off."

"Let me worry about them," Nate said. And he was. That the horses had not panicked was a miracle of no small measure. They were pulling at the picket stakes, their eyes wide, their nostrils flared.

Nate had never seen a herd come so close to a

fire. Or, for that matter, to humans. An old Shoshone once claimed that a herd passed through the man's village when the Shoshone was a boy, but Nate had always regarded the tale as a flight of fancy. Not anymore. "So long as they don't stampede we'll be fine," he whispered.

From out of the darkness came a low laugh tinged with the spite of the man who was laughing. "Can you hear me, King?"

Nate did not respond. Not with the buffalo so near.

"Of course you can," One-Eye Jackson said. "I've been here all damn day, so close I could have chucked a stone and hit you. And you never spotted me. I bet you feel mighty stupid right about now."

Nate still did not reply.

"That's all right. Don't answer me. We wouldn't want to spook all these buffs." Jackson gave vent to more laughter. "Funny how things work out, huh? Here I was, racking my brain for a way to get back at you, and look what happens. Life hands me revenge on a silver platter."

The sound of his voice was agitating the buffalo. They were grunting and snorting more loudly.

"I'm perfectly safe. A couple of minutes ago I shimmied up a tree, real careful like," Jackson said. "But you're on the ground. You and those other two. And on the ground is no place to be."

"He wouldn't!" Cynthia breathed.

"I heard that, sweet thing," One-Eye Jackson chortled. "I can't pass up a chance like this. I'd rather kill King with my own hands. But this will do just as well. Can you think of anything more horrible than being trampled to death?"

Nate broke his silence. "Not with the woman here."

"So? You think I give a damn? This is where I pay you back for letting those Shoshones cut my eyeball out."

"What will he do?" Shipley whispered.

The answer came in the form of a shriek worthy of a mountain lion.

Buffalo were fickle creatures. For all their size and strength, it did not take much to spook them. They were like horses. They frightened easily. Sometimes the crash of thunder whipped a herd into mindless flight. Other times it might be something as simple as the howl of a wolf or the brittle rattle of a rattlesnake. Indians exploited their fickle temperament by sometimes swooping down on a herd and yelling and yipping to drive the herd over a nearby bluff or cliff.

Noise was the common factor. It might be a loud noise or it might not. The shriek of a mountain lion, or a close imitation, was more than enough to ignite the flight impulse in every brute within earshot.

The instant Jackson's cry shattered the night, Nate was in motion. But he did not leap to the side of the Beechers, as might be expected. His first act was to streak his bowie from its beaded sheath and dart to the horses. Four swift slashes, and the horses were free of the picket ropes and could try to save themselves. Which they did by whinnying and galloping off in the direction the buffalo were stampeding.

Only then did Nate run to the Beechers, who had sprung to their feet and were gazing about in wide-eyed consternation.

As well they should.

Panic was spreading like a prairie wildfire. On all sides buffalo were exploding into violent motion. Within seconds the entire herd had been transformed into a frothing, roiling river of horns and hooves.

Nate had moments in which to do something. The buffalo were pressing in close, the flickering flames of the fire no longer enough to deter them. The rumble of hooves, the snorts and bellows and grunts and the crash of undergrowth, rose to a nigh-deafening din.

Shipley threw an arm around his wife. "What do we do?" he cried.

Nate glanced right and left. None of the trees were within swift reach. To try to climb one invited a horrible death. Nor would running accomplish anything other than to land them in an early grave. There was no cover to be had, no boulders or logs that might offer some slight degree of protection. They were in the open next to the spring. *The spring!* Suddenly grabbing hold of the Beechers, Nate propelled them toward it.

"See here!" Shipley blurted. "What are you—"

Nate did not stop or slacken his speed when he came to the water's edge. He hurtled into the spring, taking the husband and wife with him. The water closed about them like a clammy fist. He did not go all the way under but managed to find footing. The level only came as high as his shoulders.

Shipley and Cynthia were not as fortunate. Both sank from sight, then reappeared flailing and sputtering.

The farmer was incensed. "What the hell! Why did you do that?"

"Don't you get it?" Cynthia shouted. "He's trying to save us. Look!"

Paddling furiously to stay afloat, her husband twisted.

All around them the ground shook and rumbled. A horde of buffalo were plowing through the stand. A force of nature unleashed, the great brutes smashed into, through, and over anything and everything in their path. Vegetation was churned beneath thousands of pounding hooves. Whole thickets were reduced to pulp. Trees crashed down, uprooted like so many cat-o'-nine-tails. Clods of grass went flying.

"Dear God!" Cynthia exclaimed.

The fire went out, the brands were scattered.

All that could be seen of the buffalo were hump-backed silhouettes and the dull glint of the twin scimitars that jutted from their huge heads.

From out of that living river of sinew came several barks and a sharp yelp.

"Byron!" Cynthia cried. "I forgot about Byron!" She paddled toward the water's edge, but Shipley grabbed her and would not let go.

Dust rose, fast and thick. It became a cloud. A fog that shrouded all around them.

So far not one buffalo had plunged into the spring. Buffalo were not averse to fording rivers, but they generally avoided water. Too, the brutes had been filing past on either side when the stampede began and continued to do so, impelled by the ages-old instinct that caused the great beasts to follow one another as blindly as lemmings.

Any instant, though, that might change. And if just one of the brutes veered into the spring, others were bound to follow. The three humans would be reduced to pulverized meat and crushed bone. A possibility of which Nate King was all too keenly aware. Every nerve taut, every muscle rigid, he peered into the dust and strained his ears to catch the rush of movement that would foreshadow their end.

On and on the stampede lasted. Thousands upon thousands of buffalo pounded past.

Between the dust and the darkness, the Beechers were indistinct shapes. Cynthia leaned close to him so he would hear her and shouted, "How much longer?"

There was no telling, and Nate said so.

Some herds were small. Some were immense. This one was one of the latter. Half an hour went by. Three-quarters of an hour. Gauging the passage of time was difficult with the dust blocking out the stars.

Then came signs the stampede would soon end. The thunder, the riotous bedlam, dwindled by slow degrees until finally the herd was reduced to small clusters that in turn gave way to solitary stragglers.

Not long after, the pounding ceased. In the distance to the north the rumbling ceased. A deep and profound silence fell.

"Is it over?" Cynthia asked breathlessly.

"It seems to be, but stay put just in case." Nate started to climb out.

"Like hell," Shipley Beecher said, and scrambled ahead of him. Coughing and swatting at the dust, Shipley stood. "That was an experience I would not care to ever repeat."

Uncurling, Nate shook himself like a waterlogged bear. His buckskins and moccasins were soaked. Were he alone, he would strip and wring out his clothes.

Cynthia was trying to lever herself out of the spring. She kept slipping.

"Permit me," Nate said. Her hand was small

and warm in his. He lifted her effortlessly and steadied her once she was out. "There."

"Thank you," Cynthia said. "And thank you for saving us. If you hadn't done what you did, we would be dead."

Shipley's snort was remarkably like that of the buffalo. "Nonsense. It was the spring that saved us." He did more swatting. "Our horses have run off, but all in all, we're not in bad shape."

Nate disagreed but did not comment.

"Where did Byron get to?" Cynthia wondered. "I hope he escaped those ugly monstrosities."

Nate was thinking of One-Eye Jackson. If Jackson were still alive, he might try to catch them off-guard. Nate gripped his Hawken in both hands, then looked at it. Like his clothes, his rifle and pistols had been drenched and were dripping water. The same with his powder horn. He could not use his guns until the powder dried.

Cynthia cupped a hand to her mouth. "Byron! Byron! Come here, boy!" She started to walk off.

Grabbing her wrist, Nate said, "Stay here. And no yelling."

"I don't understand," Cynthia said. "The buffalo are gone. Why can't I look for my dog?"

"And have Jackson get his hands on you?"

"Oh."

"No one could live through that," Shipley Beecher scoffed. "It's a wonder we did. The Almighty was looking out for us."

"We should wait until daylight to look around," Nate insisted.

"Spend the rest of the night twiddling our thumbs?" Shipley said. "I should say not."

Nate was spared further argument by the drum of approaching hooves from the south. He crouched, pulling Cynthia beside him. "Get down!"

Shipley Beecher did no such thing. Instead, he turned toward the hoofbeats and shrugged free of the cord with which he had slung his rifle across his back. Tucking the stock to his shoulder, he thumbed back the hammer.

Nate opened his mouth to say the rifle would not fire.

That was when a buffalo hove out of the night.

CHAPTER FIVE

It was an old cow. Apparently she had fallen during the stampede and been trampled by her own kind. Jagged bone showed white against her lower front leg, and she bore multiple wounds. One was a long gash on her neck that oozed a copious flow of blood.

Shipley squeezed the trigger and was rewarded with a dry *click*. The cow was almost on top of him when he leaped aside.

In her weakened, dazed state, the cow had not noticed him until he moved. Startled, she veered, limping badly, and blundered into the spring. The splash was tremendous. She kicked and thrashed, sending waves sloshing. But she could not stay afloat. She was nearly spent. Her head went under, and her struggles grew weaker and weaker until finally they ceased altogether.

"Did you see?" Shipley marveled. "That brainless clod almost killed me."

Nate was more concerned about something else, but they had no means of hauling the cow out of the water. Tactfully, he said, "We would be well advised to stay where we are."

"I suppose," the farmer conceded.

The dust was thinning, but they could not see more than twenty feet. Once the water stopped sloshing, quiet reigned.

"Wait until I tell my friends that I lived through a buffalo stampede," Shipley said. "They won't believe it."

"We were lucky," Nate said.

Beecher was fiddling with his rifle. "I have dry powder on my packhorse. We should look for our animals."

"We won't find them stumbling around in the dark," Nate said.

"So we waste the entire night?" Shipley grumbled. "I think it's a mistake. We need dry powder. We need it now, before another buffalo or something else comes along. I'm going to look for them whether you want me to or not."

"You're a grown man."

"It's nice of you to notice." Shipley beckoned his wife. "Come on, Cyn. This fellow is on his own from here on out."

"No," Cynthia said softly.

"Excuse me? It is unseemly for you to stay here

by yourself. I won't have it." Shipley held out his hand to her.

"No, Ship. Mr. King is right. We won't accomplish much bumbling about in the dark. Let's do as he says and wait until we have light to see by."

"I resent this, Cyn," Ship said. "I resent it heartily."

"I'm sorry. Truly sorry. But he knows this country and we don't. We must rely on his judgment."

"Must we indeed?" Shipley archly rejoined. But he slung his rifle across his chest, and squatted. "I must say, this experience has been a revelation, and I'm not sure I like what I've learned."

"You're talking in riddles," Cynthia said. "You can't fault me for doing what I believe is best."

"You promised to love, honor, and *obey*, remember? Yet, one of the few times I insist, you refuse."

"Please, Ship," Cynthia said. "This is hardly the time for a spat. I love you as dearly as ever. But I don't always agree with your decisions, and this is one of those I don't agree with."

Nate was tired of their squabbling. To put a stop to it, he interjected, "Why not tell Jackson exactly where you are?"

"What can he do without weapons?" Shipley said curtly. But he quit his carping.

The rest of the night was a grueling test of nerves and will. Nate refused to fall asleep, but along about three in the morning, he did. Not for long, no more than half an hour, but he was annoyed by his lapse.

A pink tinge in the eastern sky brought a sense of relief. But Nate did not relax his vigilance, not when the pink became gold, nor when a blazing yellow crown rested on the world's shoulders.

Shipley and Cynthia had been sleeping for hours. Cynthia awoke first, and blinked in astonishment. "Where did everything go?"

Except for about a dozen of the larger cottonwoods, the island of vegetation in the sea of grass was no more. In its place was trampled earth, bare soil pockmarked with thousands upon thousands of hoofprints. The undergrowth—every bush, every plant—had been pulverized to bits and swept away as if by a giant broom. Here and there were the splintered remnants of toppled trees. The birds that had roosted in those trees were gone, the small creatures that had made their homes in the underbrush had fled or been trampled.

Dust covered everything. It covered Nate and the farmer and his wife. It covered the dead cow that floated in the spring, and choked the water. Once so pure, the spring was now a reddish brown; a brown from the dust and red from the cow's blood.

Drawing his tomahawk, Nate waded in to his shins and chopped off a good-sized piece of flank.

"What on earth are you doing?" Shipley Beecher asked.

"Breakfast."

"I don't know as I'm hungry."

"Me either," Cynthia said.

But both ate their ample share after Nate roasted the meat. While they were wiping their fingers on their clothes, he waded back in and chopped off another sizable piece and a strip of hide to wrap it in.

Shipley pointed at the hide. "You're taking some with us?"

"Unless you would rather starve."

"Which way do we go?" Cynthia asked. "We won't last long without our provisions."

"Stay calm," Ship said. "It's not as bad as it seems."

No, it's worse, Nate almost said aloud. Their horses were gone. They were stranded. Their source of water had been fouled. The haunch he was taking would not last long. Their powder was still wet, so their guns were still useless. As if that were not enough, they were in the heart of hostile territory. Comanche country, no less. And they had a white enemy to deal with.

"Is there any sign of Byron?" Cynthia asked.

Nate gazed at the stub of a cottonwood trunk a ways off. Beside it, caked with dirt, was part of a canine skull. A freshly caved-in skull, the brain partly visible. In a way the dog was the lucky one. It had died a quick death. Which was more than might be said for them. "I haven't seen him," he fibbed, hoping she would not notice it.

"I hope he got away."

Shouldering the Hawken, Nate turned north and began walking. He did not let himself dwell on how far it was to Bent's Fort.

"Wait, Mr. King." Cynthia caught up and matched his pace. "I want the truth about something." She waited for an acknowledgment that was not offered. "I sense you are upset."

"It's nothing your husband can't fix."

"Ship can be a trial, I admit. But he's a good person at heart. Once you get to know him better, you'll see."

"If you say so." Nate was saving his breath for hiking.

"My husband likes to do things his way, is all," Cynthia explained. "He always has."

"And you always let him."

"That's harsh," Cynthia said. "I won't deny he is hardheaded. But deep down he is a peach or I wouldn't have married him."

Nate glanced over his shoulder. Shipley was a dozen yards back, slouching along like a petulant child. "Was that what you wanted to ask about?"

"No. I want to know what our chances are. Don't sugarcoat it. I won't fall to pieces."

"I won't lie. They aren't good," Nate confessed. No sense, he thought, in mentioning the hurdles they must overcome. He squinted at the sun, dreading when the heat would worsen.

"In other words, you have doubts we'll make it. But surely the three of us, working together, will survive?"

"We can try out best," Nate said.

Thankfully, Cynthia did not talk his head off but settled down to hour after hour of steady plodding. They started out strong, but by noon the prairie was an inferno in the fiery grip of its relentless mistress. Sweat poured from their bodies, and their throats were parched. Shipley cursed cow buffaloes.

The afternoon was everything Nate feared it would be. The heat was relentless. It came off the prairie in blistering waves, plastering his buckskins to his body. But he did not mind the burden of the meat. It gained them another day of life.

They saw no trace of buffalo other than a dead calf that had slipped and been mangled. They also came across a dead rabbit, or what little was left of it, and the front half of a doe.

The Beechers did not have much to say. Shipley, in particular, was a human clam. Whenever Nate glanced at him, the farmer looked away.

Nate was in superb condition, but even he dragged his heels by sunset. His legs were leaden. He longed for a drink of water. Just one cool, refreshing drink.

Grass had to suffice for their fire, but it burned too quickly. They had to constantly add more. They were so famished, they tore into the haunch before it was halfway cooked, and didn't care.

The Beechers did not have much to say to one another, which was just as well. Another evening of their prattle would test Nate's self-control.

It was about eight o'clock when Nate opened his powder horn and poured a thimble-full into his palm. The powder felt dry to the touch, but he had to be sure. He reloaded the Hawken. He started by flipping the frizzen open and ensuring that the hammer was forward. Next he poured powder from the powder horn down the barrel. Taking a ball from his ammo pouch, he wrapped it in a patch. He fed the patch and ball into the barrel, tamping them down with the ramrod. He charged the pan with powder, adding no more than half a pan, and flipped the frizzen back.

Shipley watched with interest. "If your powder works, mine will too."

Nate checked the flint. He thumbed back the hammer. He pulled the rear trigger to set the front trigger. Other than grass, grass, and more grass, there was nothing to shoot at, so he aimed at a clump fifty yards from where he stood, and fired. He was rewarded with a *crack* and the belch of smoke and lead, and part of the clump dissolved in a spray of dirt.

"Now we can hunt and defend ourselves," Shipley said happily, unslinging his rifle.

Nate reloaded his Hawken yet again. He inspected and reloaded one of his pistols. He was replacing the powder in the second pistol when Cynthia Beecher cleared her throat.

"I hope you won't mind my saying, but I'm surprised you still use flintlocks. I don't know a lot about firearms, but I do know that percussion models have been popular for a while now."

Nate shrugged. "Flintlocks are what I'm used to."

"I'm the same way," Shipley interjected. "Although my uncle and my cousin have been wanting me to switch for a few years now. They say it's easier and faster to reload a percussion than a flintlock."

"It's worth looking into," Cynthia stressed.

Nate realized she was attempting to be helpful, so he smiled and said, "Maybe I will on my next visit to St. Louis." He bought all his firearms from the Hawken brothers, and he trusted their workmanship.

Presently, the firmament sparkled with a myriad of stars, the spectacle made all the more dazzling by the rising of a full moon. A moon so big and bright, it lent the illusion they could reach out and touch it.

"How beautiful!" Cynthia breathed. "We never had moons like this back in Indiana. I wonder why that should be."

"I talked to a man once who said it had something to do with the atmosphere," Nate related. He gestured at the heavenly body. "A lot of plains tribes call this the Thunder Moon."

"The Indians give the moon names?"

"What we call January, most tribes call the Cold Moon. February is the Hunger Moon. Some tribes called March the Crow Moon. Others call it the Waking Moon. April is known as the Grass Moon and the Geese Moon—"

"Let me guess," Cynthia interrupted. "Because that's when the geese fly north again?"

Nate nodded. "May is the Planting Moon. June is the Buck Moon, or Rose Moon. Then there is the Heat Moon, or Blood Moon, depending on the tribe. Which brings us to the Thunder Moon. Or, as some tribes in the northwest call it, the Sturgeon Moon."

"Too many moons for me to remember them all," Cynthia said.

"The Thunder Moon has a third name," Nate said. "Some call it the Comanche Moon. It's the time of year when the Comanches range far and wide in search of throats to slit. White throats, mostly."

Shipley sniffed in irritation. "Did you have to bring that up and frighten my wife half to death?"

"I mentioned it for your sake, too," Nate informed him. "This is the time of year when we are most likely to run into a Comanche war party."

"Let them come," Shipley Beecher said. "I'll teach them to have respect for their betters."

The five came north again. As before, it was Nocona's idea. As before, Pahkah of the crooked nose, wise old Soko, Sargento the bloodthirsty, and Howeah, who seldom talked, were with him.

But this time they did not come to hunt. This time they had painted black stripes across their foreheads and the lower part of their cheeks. This time they were on the warpath.

They had been riding for many sleeps. They crossed the sign of a band of Kiowa-Apaches, but the Kiowas were their friends. They crossed Cheyenne sign, but ever since a special council, the Comanches had been at peace with the Cheyenne. They crossed Arapaho sign, but the Arapahos were allies of the Cheyenne.

The sign the five Wasps sought most, they did not find. The sign of those the Nemene yearned to destroy. The sign of white men.

Came the day when wise Soko gave voice to the thought of all. "We have come far and not found those we seek. We should return to our people."

"Go back without counting coup?" Pahkah said.

"Without a single scalp?" Sargento added.

"I share your disappointment," Nocona assured them. "So I say we ride north for seven more sleeps. If we have not found whites by then, we will wipe the paint from our faces."

The others agreed.

For six days they pushed north. On the seventh morning they came on buffalo sign. It was old, that of a large herd. The tracks showed where the herd had stampeded.

Late that afternoon, just when Nocona was about to suggest they stop for the day and head back at first light, a putrid odor was borne to their nostrils.

"A dead buffalo," Sargento guessed.

"The meat will be bad," Soko said.

They rode a little farther and discovered a spring and a badly bloated and severely decomposed cow. "It is an omen," Nocona announced. "This is as far as we go."

Sargento was riding around the spring idly examining tracks, when he hauled on the reins to his warhorse, threw back his head, and whooped. "The cow is an omen, but not the omen you think!"

One look, and excitement coursed through all of them. Excitement at the prospect of the hunt.

"Spread out," Nocona said. "See what else we can find."

They were thorough. They took their time. When they were done, they gathered to compare observations.

"Four whites, one of them a woman," Soko concluded, "and a dog."

"The dog is dead," Howeah said.

"Two of the whites and the woman have gone north on foot," Sargento said. For once he was cheerful. He liked nothing better than shedding white blood.

"The fate of the third white man is a mystery," Pahkah said. "His tracks do not leave with the rest."

"We take the scalps of the other two," Sargento

said. "The woman I will keep for my own. Beating her each morning will give me much pleasure."

"We will decide later about the woman," Nocona said. "First we must catch them. They are on foot, but they are seven to ten sleeps ahead of us."

"We can catch them in half that time," Sargento predicted.

"Then no one objects?" Nocona asked. "We hunt them?"

All were agreed.

New vitality in their veins, they pushed north. But that afternoon the unexpected dampened their mood. They came on a prairie dog town. The prairie dogs whistled and scattered, and the five Wasps threaded through the burrows with the casual care of men who had done it many times and never suffered a mishap. They suffered one this day.

Pahkah's horse had the misfortune to have the ground give way under its weight. Pahkah had swung wide of a burrow, unaware it angled sharply and was close to the surface. The earth buckled and his mount's front leg plunged into the hole. Pahkah was thrown. In midair he heard—they all heard—the horrendous *crunch*, and his mount's shrill whinny.

The leg was broken. Shattered in two places.

The five Nemene stood in a circle around the stricken animal. It was Pahkah's warhorse, but all of them shared in his sorrow at what had to be done. They were not Apaches. They did not regard horses as food on the hoof. Especially their war mounts, the best of their herds. Often, when enemies were sighted near their village, they took their warhorses into their lodges so their enemies could not steal them. To the Nemene, their warhorse was their most valued possession. So when Pahkah drew his knife and silently, mercifully, slit the animal's throat, they looked on in respectful silence.

Pahkah dipped a finger in the gushing blood and added red lines to each cheek. "I raised him from a colt."

Soko offered to let Pahkah ride double.

Howeah commented that the death of the horse might be another omen. No one had anything to say to that.

Soon they rode on, more somber than they had been. That night they made a cold camp. Soko talked about how it had been in the old days, before the coming of the white blight. The others had heard his account many times but they listened in rapt attention. Every man there longed for a return of the old ways, for a time when the whites were erased from their world.

The next morning, another delay.

They awoke to find that two of the horses had strayed off. A remarkable circumstance. It had never happened before due to their habit of sleeping with the reins of their animals wrapped around a wrist or ankle. Yet both Sargento's and Howeah's mounts were gone. They found no evidence enemies were to blame. The animals had simply wandered away.

Half the morning was spent tracking them down. Pahkah rode double with Soko and Howeah rode double with Nocona. Sargento loped at their side, his swarthy features made darker by his anger at the delay. Had his missing horse not been his favorite of favorites, it would have suffered the same fate as Pahkah's unfortunate mount.

They caught the horses without much problem once they found them. Howeah had to talk soothingly to his before it would let him touch it. He said that the horses running off was another omen, to which Sargento snapped, "You see omens in everything."

The next day they came on new sign, and it puzzled them. They followed the maker of the sign awhile, digesting the tidbits of information the tracks revealed, and at length they drew rein to consult.

"It is one of the white men," Nocona said, "and four horses."

"He came from the east," Pahkah said, "and struck the trail of the whites who are on foot."

"Now he follows them," Sargento said.

"But he is not in a hurry to catch them," Soko said. "He goes no faster than they do. It is strange."

"They are white," Sargento said, implying that was sufficient to explain any and all strangeness.

"One of the horses is heavy with packs," Howeah mentioned. "Our women will be pleased."

Sargento smirked. "You always think of your woman."

"Are you saying I think of her too much?" Howeah replied.

Nocona was quick to intervene. "Our women can wait. Our people can wait. Our minds must be on the whites and only the whites. There are more of us, but they are bound to have guns."

"Were it not for their guns," Sargento said, "the whites would have been driven into the sea."

Nocona slapped his legs against his warhorse.

They were eager, but they were not reckless. They did not goad their animals to the point of exhaustion. Not as hot as it was. Not with two of them riding double.

That evening Soko dropped a rabbit with an arrow, a spectacular shot. The shaft sliced into the rabbit in midbound at a distance some of the younger warriors would not attempt.

They ate well, washing the juicy meat down with water from their water skins. They washed it down sparingly.

Later that night, as they lay talking, Howeah suddenly sat up and pointed. "There."

A blazing streak pierced the heavens.

"A fire star!" Nocona declared.

"The best omen of all," Pahkah said.

Sargento grunted in pleasure. "The whites we chase do not know it, but they will all soon be dead."

CHAPTER SIX

Day after day of plodding north. Day after day of the relentless burning heat. Day after day without sign of water. No streams, no springs, no rivers, nothing but the grass and the hard earth underfoot. The three of them would have died of thirst if not for Nate King.

Dew saved them. Following Nate's instructions, each morning at sunrise they soaked up the dew with strips of buckskin or cloth. It was never much. No more than a few handfuls. But those precious handfuls kept them alive. They supplied them with barely enough water to make it through the day.

Hunger was more readily solved. They had their rifles and pistols, and game was abundant. But deer usually fled before they were in range, and smaller game proved frustratingly elusive. Shipley tried again and again to bring something down but could not. Once again, Nate King saved them. He seldom missed. When Shipley asked the secret to his success, Nate replied, "Stalk as close as you can and never fire until you are sure."

Cynthia grew increasingly quiet the farther they traveled. It got so Shipley repeatedly asked if she was all right. "You're not acting like yourself," was his assessment.

To his many probes, Cynthia Beecher said she was fine. "Just worn out, is all. I don't have breath to spare for chatter."

Shipley was satisfied, but Nate was troubled. The very next night, after Shipley had fallen asleep, Nate was taking his turn at keeping watch, sitting off by himself, when the grass rustled and the farmer's wife sat down next to him. She did not say anything for a while, and he did not ask why she was there. He figured she would get around to telling him.

"Do you ever make mistakes?"

The whispered query was not entirely unexpected. Nate answered, "All the time. It keeps me humble."

"You make very few, in my estimation. If not for you, we would long since have died."

"I've had a lot of practice at this," Nate said. "When you must either live off the land or die, you learn to live off the land."

"It's more than that," Cynthia whispered. Her

face was lovely in the moonlight, her hair as lustrous as corn silk. "You have a competence about you that is more than the sum of your experience."

"If you say so," Nate said, making light of it.

"You know what I am getting at, don't you? I'm having second thoughts. Feelings I never thought I would feel."

Nate pretended to be interested in the stars.

"He's always been adequate. More than adequate in many regards. But ever since the incident with that scoundrel Jackson, I see him through new eyes. And I do not entirely like what I see."

"You're being too hard on yourself, and on him."

"Maybe. Maybe not. Maybe he's not the man I thought he was. Maybe hitching my apron to him was a mistake."

Despite a cool breeze out of the northwest, Nate's skin became unusually warm. "You shouldn't talk like that. You took a vow."

"That is what keeps me in line," Cynthia whispered. She was staring at him, not the stars. "But I am more disenchanted every day, and I fear that before much more time goes by, the disenchantment will be complete."

"If you look for something you will find it."

"I know, I know. But I can't help how I feel. A woman likes her man to be equal to every occasion, and he has fallen short."

Nate tore his gaze from the heavens. "No man can predict every happenstance. The best we can do is adapt."

"You adapt extraordinarily well. Ship does not."

"You're being unfair. He's never been west of the Mississippi, yet you expect him to be an expert."

"Not necessarily," Cynthia hedged. "I just expect him not to get me killed."

The breeze gusted, and Nate sniffed the wind, hoping for a hint of moisture, but there was none. She did not speak so he did not, either. For a while, anyway.

"I admit, I'm confused."

"The confusion will pass," Nate said. He was uncomfortable, but he did not shoo her off. He wanted to clear the air. Her next broadside only clouded it.

"Is it possible to love two people at once?"

"Not the way you mean," Nate said. He avoided meeting her gaze. The inner power females possessed was formidable.

"How do you know? Has it ever happened to you? I am torn in two directions, and I don't know what to do."

"Do nothing," Nate said.

"I've always thought that women who felt like this were fickle. That they were weak inside. I looked down my nose at them, I am ashamed to admit. Now that I'm in their shoes, I see I was wrong. It's not whimsy. It's not being weak. It's the human heart."

Nate saw his opening. "There is only room in my heart for one. There will only ever be room for one."

"Now who is predicting?" Cynthia jousted. "I sense you are afraid to admit the truth."

"Your truth is not the same as mine," Nate said flatly. "Your heart is not my heart."

"Point taken," Cynthia conceded. "But it doesn't change how I feel, and that is what it always comes back to. Feelings."

"They will fade in time," Nate said. "Infatuations always do."

"Is that what you think this is? A girlish lark? I am a grown woman."

"And a husband you took to your womanly bosom. That is the core. That is the crux. That is the truth above all other truths." Nate thought he had settled it. He forgot the feminine penchant for a flank attack.

"How is it you turn a phrase so nicely? You did not learn that trapping beaver or slaying grizzlies."

Nate did not want to, but he grinned. "I read a lot. I collect books. I have a library. Not much of one, since many of them were destroyed not long ago. But I am rebuilding it, slowly but surely."

"You have more between your ears than most," Cynthia whispered. "I saw it in your eyes the day we met."

"Your husband is no slouch," Nate rallied.

"He is no poet, either. He doesn't like to read. Never has. Books bore him. He would rather be doing something than sit and read."

Nate forgot himself. Reading was his passion,

and he could not let it go undefended. "Has he ever tried *The Iliad*? Or *The Deerslayer*? Books have a life of their own. They take us to other times, other places. They let us see life through other eyes. They widen our own sight."

Cynthia smiled. "Nicely put, and a perfect example of what I have been talking about."

"The thing is," Nate said, deciding it had gone on long enough, "I am spoken for. Above and before all else, I am spoken for."

"A woman can always dream," Cynthia said softly.

Nate went at it along another path. "He would die for you."

"And you would not?"

"I would protect you as I would protect anyone. There is a difference. To him, you are everything. You are the reason he wakes up in the morning, the reason he wants more land. He has risked his life to make you happy."

"He has risked my life, as well."

"At your insistence, I understand," Nate said. "He asked you to stay in Indiana. You refused. You nearly lost your life, yes, but the losing is your doing, not his."

"You have a gallant soul, Nathaniel King."

Of the sundry female wiles, it was the straightforward thrust Nate was most susceptible to, and he knew it. With that in mind, he replied, "I'm as ordinary as dirt."

Cynthia started to reply but recoiled as if she

had been slapped at the very instant that metal touched the nape of Nate's neck.

"If I listen to much more of this, I will vomit. Keep your hands where they are, King. As for you, wench, yell for help and I will blow this gallant soul's head off." One-Eye Jackson snickered.

Nate boiled with fury. Not at Jackson but at himself for letting himself be distracted. His lapse might cost them their lives.

"I can't believe how easy you made it." One-Eye rubbed salt in the wound. "The mighty Grizzly Killer. Taken by surprise because some filly is making cow-eyes at him. And a married filly, at that. I must remember to look up your Shoshone squaw and tell her about your little romance."

Nate's fury increased tenfold. He almost lost his hold over himself, almost whirled to attack Jackson even though the outcome was not in doubt. Jackson's reflexes were the equal of his, and Jackson had no qualms about squeezing the trigger.

"My, my. Look at you tremble," One-Eye taunted. "Must be a nip in the air." He chuckled, then said, "Woman, listen good. I want you to relieve Mr. King, here, of his armory. Stand where I can see you. Toss his rifle and both his pistols out of reach. The same with his pigsticker and the tomahawk."

"If I refuse?"

"Why, then, I shoot him and gut you and then shoot your husband when he rushes to your rescue."

"You are despicable."

"Hell, lady, I'll gladly lay claim to being scum if that will make you happy. You see, unlike you, I'm not hampered by scruples." One-Eye paused. "Then again, you must not have any either or you wouldn't be pouring your heart out to Grizzly Killer while your husband snores not twenty feet away."

"I hate you," Cynthia said.

"I'm flattered. I'm a good hater, myself. I've hated this big tub of righteousness for years now."

"What did he ever do to you?"

One-Eye's voice lost its humor. "Know what? You ask too damn many questions. Do as I told you and be damn quick about it or I'll damn well kill the two of you for the damn well hell of it."

"You swear too much," Cynthia said, turning toward Nate with arms out from her sides.

That struck One-Eye as hilarious. He broke into a belly laugh but stifled it and said, "You sure do amuse me, Mrs. Beecher. Maybe I'll take you with me. How would that be? The two of us, alone, with all these warm nights to while away?"

"I would rather be burned alive." Cynthia slid a flintlock from under Nate's belt and threw it into the grass.

"I haven't kissed you yet. You might grow to like it."

Nate dearly yearned to end Jackson's gloating, but the pressure of the muzzle on his neck did not slacken. "Quit insulting her," he said, and received a hard blow to the back of his head that nearly blacked him out.

"Did I say you could talk? Keep your mouth shut if you know what's good for you. I'm hankering to pull this trigger like I've never hankered after anything in all my born days." Jackson gouged the barrel hard into Nate's neck. "You cost me my eye, you son of a bitch."

Risking another blow, Nate said, "It always comes back to that. And you always have it wrong. *You* cost yourself the eye. I just happened to be there."

For perhaps half a minute Jackson did not respond. Then he said with icy reserve, "Ever pull the legs off grasshoppers when you were a sprout? Or cut a snake and put it on an anthill?"

"Can't say as I did, no."

"You missed out. My point is that making you suffer will be one of the great joys of my life. I don't want you to die quick. That would upset me something awful."

Cynthia stepped back. She had done as Jackson had commanded. "What now?" she asked. "Do I bind him for you since you're too cowardly to do it yourself?"

"My dear woman," One-Eye said with a grin, "your childish barbs are wasted on hide as thick as mine." He sidled to the left where he could watch them both. "Now, what say we waltz over and ask your husband how-does-he-do?"

Nate's head was throbbing. He gauged the distance between them but did not resist.

Shipley Beecher was on his back, his head on his saddle, doing a remarkable imitation of a bull elk bugling. He stirred when Jackson kicked his leg but did not wake up.

"This idiot wouldn't last two seconds in Apache country," One-Eye remarked. He kicked Beecher again, in the ribs.

The farmer came out from under his blanket in befuddlement. "What in the world? Who did that to me?"

One-Eye pointed his rifle at Shipley. "Not the sharpest of razors, are you? Throw up your hands or be shot."

It always took Beecher several minutes to rouse from slumber. He was one of those who could not wake up quickly if his life depended on it. Unfortunately for him, in this instance it did. Instead of throwing up hands, he stared in confusion at his wife, then at Nate, and finally at Jackson. Understanding filled his eyes, even as his hand flashed for a pistol.

One-Eye shot him.

Chance had thrown an opportunity at Nate, and he took it. Spinning, he threw himself at Jackson. He counted on being able to reach him before Jackson unlimbered a pistol. He was wrong.

A flintlock blossomed as if out of thin air, trained on Nate's middle. Bracing for the agony of being gut-shot, Nate drew up short. It saved his life. One-Eye had the hammer curled back, but he did not squeeze the trigger.

"That's close enough."

Shipley was on the ground, thrashing and gritting his teeth, a hand over the wound in his right shoulder. He did not handle pain well. He cursed. He mewed. He made inarticulate sounds.

"What an infant," One-Eye said. "He should be ashamed to wear britches." Suddenly tensing, he demanded, "What do you think you're doing?"

Cynthia had dropped to her knees beside Shipley. Clutching his other arm, she said, "Calm down, Ship! Calm down! You're still alive and there's not much blood. You'll live."

One-Eye Jackson laughed. "Isn't she the optimist?" He moved back a few steps, the better to cover them. "Now then. Suppose we get to it? Woman, I want you to fetch the horses. Walk south about two hundred yards and you'll find where I tethered them."

"You honestly expect me to bring them back here?"

"I expect you want your husband and your mountain man to live," One-Eye answered. "So you'll bring the horses, yes, and you won't dawdle, or I'll put lead into the two of them. Which will it be?"

Her back stiff in resentment, her small fists clenched, Cynthia marched off to do his bidding.

"Don't get eaten by a bear!" One-Eye hollered after her.

Shipley had stopped thrashing and groaning and was glaring at the lanky frontiersman. "If it's the last thing I ever do, I will plant you."

Unfazed, Jackson responded, "Go ahead. Vent your spleen while you can. Because in an all-too-short while, neither you nor King will have tongues to vent anything with."

"What do you mean?"

One-Eye winked his good eye at Nate. "Isn't he precious? Have you ever met anyone so stupid?"

"Why are you doing this to us?" Shipley Beecher asked.

Bobbing his chin at Nate, One-Eye said, "Ask him."

The farmer shifted. "Well? Are you mute? Have the courtesy to make sense of this madness."

"I have nothing to say," Nate said.

One-Eye laughed coldly. "Guilty conscience? Have you been able to sleep at night? I haven't. I have lain awake thinking of all the wonderful ways I could pay you back. They all had one thing in common. Would you like to know what it was?"

"You'll tell me anyway."

"Smart coon." One-Eye grinned, and sobered. "The one thing they had in common was making you suffer as no man has ever suffered since the dawn of creation."

"You hate me that much?" Nate asked.

"I hate you with every breath I take. I hate you with all I am. I hate you more than any hate that has ever been, and I will go on hating you until the day you die, or I do. Is that enough hate for you?"

"All these years," Nate said.

"Every minute of every day of all those years," One-Eye amended. "And tomorrow my dream comes true. Tomorrow all those sleepless nights will be paid for in full."

Nate suppressed a smile. Jackson had inadvertently let it slip that they would live out the night. It was only about eleven. Six hours until dawn. Six hours to turn the tables.

Shipley Beecher was saying, "I don't understand. If you have hated him for so long, why haven't you acted before now?"

"I have my reasons," One-Eye said a trifle defensively.

"He could have died of old age before you got around to taking your revenge," Shipley persisted.

"Stupid, stupid, stupid," One-Eye said.

The farmer did not know when to stay quiet. "The only reason I can think of, the only reason that makes any kind of sense, is that you're scared of him."

"What?"

"Are you hard of hearing? You must be scared of him. So scared, you couldn't bring yourself to confront him."

"First your wife, now you," One-Eye said. Taking two swift strides, he smashed the stock of his rifle against Beecher's head. There was no warning, no chance for the farmer to defend himself.

Beecher folded, and One-Eye went to bash him again.

Nate started to take a step and found himself staring down the muzzle of the rifle.

"Don't be as stupid as him," One-Eye rasped.

"You won't shoot me," Nate bluffed. "You need me alive. You can't torture a dead man."

"True," One-Eye admitted. "But I can put a hole in your hip or your kneecap and still torture you to my heart's content."

Nate stayed where he was.

"That's what I thought," One-Eye said smugly. He backed off a couple of steps, then irritably growled, "What's taking that female so long? She should have been back by now."

"Two hundred yards is a long way in the dark," Nate said.

"Not if you have any sand." One-Eye peered to the south, his brow puckered. "Maybe she's up to something. Maybe she thinks she can trick me."

Nate indicated the prone form in the grass. "She won't do anything to endanger him."

"Let's hope not. Because if she does, after I'm done with you and the idiot, I'll do her in ways she has never been done." One-Eye chortled lecherously.

"You're fond of making threats," Nate observed.

"So what? I almost always carry them out." One-Eye began to pace. "I swear, if she doesn't show her pretty hide soon, I'm liable to get mad."

Nate had met more than a few men who liked

to hear the sound of their own voices, but few had been as enamored of their babble as Jackson. "Give her a few more minutes. It can't hurt."

The sound of hooves shut off whatever retort One-Eye was about to make. "Finally!" he snarled.

Cynthia was riding her horse and leading her husband's, Jackson's, and the pack animal. Reining up, she swung her leg over the pommel and slid to the ground. "Here they are."

"Did you come by way of China?" One-Eye snapped.

"Where's my bay?" Nate asked.

"How in hell should I know? It's a miracle I stumbled on these after the stampede. I never saw any sign of yours."

Cynthia saw her husband, and gasped. "Ship!" Bounding over, she knelt and clasped him to her. "What have you done to him now, you fiend?"

"I rattled the pea he uses for a brain," One-Eye sneered. "What you see in that tree stump is beyond me."

"My sweet Ship," Cynthia said, and commenced crying. A few tears that turned into a torrent.

"Enough of your blubbering," One-Eye snarled. "I swear, women are nothing but a vexation. I'm about ready to give you the same treatment I gave him."

Nate was being ignored. He slid his right foot a few inches forward, then his left. Bunching both legs, he prepared to spring.

But Jackson had the instincts of a puma. Whirling, he leveled his rifle. "Oh-ho! Nice try. Which will it be? Die now defending this cow? Or die slowly tomorrow? I'll leave it up to you."

Nate straightened. He was tired of the cat and mouse, but he would choose life every time.

"You have no idea how happy you just made me," One-Eye Jackson said, and laughed.

CHAPTER SEVEN

Dawn had long been one of Nate's two favorite times of the day. The other was evening, when the day's work was done and his family gathered in their cabin to eat supper, relax, and rest. Some of his fondest memories were of those quiet hours when Winona sat in the rocking chair in front of the fireplace and sewed or knit while his son and daughter listened to him read.

Dawn was special for a different reason. Dawn was the start of a new day. It instilled a sense of renewal, of the pulsing beat of life reborn. He would stand on his doorstep and watch the sky slowly brighten and listen to the forest fill with the chorus of bird and animal cries that betokened a profound yet simple truth. Life was for living.

But on this particular day, Nate did not look

forward to the dawn. This was one morning where he dreaded the rising sun and the heat the sun would bring with it. Because that heat might well kill him.

Nate was flat on his back, his arms and legs spread-eagle, his wrists and ankles lashed to imbedded stakes. He had been stripped to the waist and his feet were bare. A few yards to his right, Shipley Beecher was staked out.

It was One-Eye's devious doing. The wily Jackson had made the farmer pound in the stakes and tie Nate down, then had Cynthia do the same to her husband, all the while Jackson stood back covering them with his rifle. They had balked, of course, and One-Eye had threatened to shoot Nate and Shipley. When they still refused, One-Eye threatened to shoot Cynthia.

Now here they were, tied and at Jackson's mercy, with the new day about to break.

Cynthia was over by the horses, huddled in despair, her arms around her knees, her forehead on her arms.

Nate thought he heard her weeping a while ago, but he could not be sure.

As for the cause of their misery, One-Eye Jackson bubbled with sadistic glee. He walked around and around them, baring his teeth as a wolf would bare its fangs, and chortled. When a ruddy glow tinted the eastern sky, he stopped pacing and stood over Nate. "Ready for the last day of your life?"

Nate did not answer.

"Then again, you're tough as rawhide," One-Eye said. "You might last two, even three days. I hope so. The longer you last, the more you suffer."

"Let the farmer and his wife go."

One-Eye sighed. "Not that again. You've asked a dozen times. They die too. The simpleton, there, won't last as long as you because he's weak. The woman, well, let's just say I have special plans for her." He licked his thin lips.

"I should have hunted you down and killed you long ago," Nate said with keen regret.

"Not you," One-Eye scoffed. "Not the high and mighty Nate King, who always has to do what's right, even if it costs another man his eye."

"I had to tell them."

Jackson's grin vanished and his features contorted in rage. "Like hell! You could have kept your mouth shut! No one would ever have known, and I would still have both eyes."

Shipley Beecher was listening. "Tell who what? Does this have to do with whatever brought you to hating King so much?"

"It has everything to do with it," One-Eye snapped. "I lose my eye because of this self-righteous hypocrite."

"Hypocrite? You're wrong, there. King strikes me as being an honorable man."

"Oh, does he really?" One-Eye responded, and turned. "Was he being *honorable* when he was making love to your wife?"

"What?"

"Oh, that's right. You were asleep. You didn't hear them. I did, and it about made me sick."

Shipley raised his head as high as he could. "You're a liar. My wife would never betray my trust."

One-Eye chuckled. "She's a woman, isn't she? And women are as changeable as the weather. Her exact words, as best I can recollect, was that she sees you through new eyes. You're not the man she thought you were. She even told him that hitching her apron to you was a mistake."

It had grown light enough for Nate to see the farmer's expression when Shipley looked toward Cynthia. It was the expression of a man whose innards had been ripped out.

"Cyn? Is what he's saying true?"

The huddled form by the horses did not move.

"Look at her," One-Eye said. "Pretending she doesn't hear you. Or maybe she's afraid to answer, afraid to admit the truth." He laughed. "Shall I go on? Shall I tell you the rest? How she is disenchanted with you? How her disenchantment grows each and every day?"

"This can't be happening," Shipley said.

"There's more. You're no poet, I hear. But King, he's wonderful. He has more between his ears than you do."

Shipley sank back and closed his eyes. "I don't care to hear any more."

"I don't blame you. But you know I'm telling the truth. While you slept, your woman was trying to crawl into Nate King's pants."

A shriek rent the air. None of them had noticed Cynthia rise. None of them had seen her suddenly hurl herself at Jackson. One-Eye spun just as she reached him. He swung his rifle behind him, apparently thinking she might try to wrest it from him, but she went for his face instead, raking it with her fingernails while screeching at the top of her lungs.

"No! No! No! No! No!"

Jackson nearly went down. He brought up his other arm to protect himself, but it was not enough. Cynthia opened his cheek, almost scratched out his other eye. He was forced to let go of his rifle and raise his other arm to ward her off. But she would not be denied. She pressed him, a she-cat on a rampage, her nails flicking, tearing. It was a wild, insane, glorious attempt, and if she had kept her head, if she had gone for his throat, she might have brought him down. As it was, she drove him back half a dozen feet before he recovered his wits. Balling his right fist, he caught her a good one on the point of her jaw and crumpled her like paper.

"Damn you, bitch! Damn you, you stinking bitch!"

One-Eye was breathing raggedly. Crimson furrows marked his left cheek and forehead. A deep scratch was a hair's width from his eye. He glared at Cynthia, then hauled off and kicked her in the side, not once but several times.

"Stop that!" Shipley Beecher cried.

One-Eye looked up. "You'd defend her after what she did? Are you that much the simpleton?"

"I don't know whether she did or she didn't," Shipley replied. "She's down and helpless. Leave her be."

"Remarkable," One-Eye said. "Truly remarkable. If I live to be a hundred, I will never understand how people can be so dumb."

"You've never been in love," Shipley said.

"That's where you're wrong. I had a woman once. A woman as pretty as yours. A Shoshone."

"King's wife is a Shoshone."

"That's right. I met her back when I had two eyes. The woman I was with belonged to the same band." One-Eye stopped and stared at the ground. "Little Fawn was her name." He fell silent and stood as still as a statue.

A groan from Cynthia goaded One-Eye into walking over and nudging her, hard. "Get up."

"Can't you see she's unconscious?" Shipley yelled. "Haven't you hurt her enough?"

"Mister, I haven't even started." One-Eye strode to his horse and returned with a length of rope. He tied Cynthia's wrists behind her back, then kicked her and came over to Nate. "Didn't think I'd forgotten about you, I trust."

"No such luck," Nate said.

The sun crowned the horizon. Already, the mild chill of the night was giving way to the warmth of the new day. Warmth that would soon transform the prairie into hell on earth.

Jackson set his rifle down and slowly drew his bone-handled knife. His eyes glittering with the lust to inflict pain and suffering, he hunkered and smiled. "Well now. Where to begin?"

Nate focused on a pillowy cloud high in the azure vault.

"I aim to whittle on you awhile. Maybe cut off a few fingers and toes. Or how about your nose? Your wife won't think you're so handsome then, will she? Not that she will ever see you again." One-Eye waited, then asked, "Nothing to say? You flapped your gums in the village that day. Remember?"

"I had to tell them."

"Sure you did. Up there on your pedestal, looking down your nose at the rest of us. You had to butt in. You had to turn them against me."

"They let you live," Nate said.

One-Eye hissed and poised the tip of his blade over Nate's chest. "Is that what they told you? That they let me go out of the goodness of their hearts? Stinking savages. I escaped. I passed out and they left me alone in the lodge. They didn't reckon on me reviving so quickly. They had tied me up, but I had a knife hid under my legging. I cut the rope, made a slit in the back of the lodge, and lit a shuck before that cousin of your wife's came back to finish me."

"I didn't know that," Nate admitted.

"Did the Shoshones tell you what they did to me?"

"They showed me your eye."

"And what did you do? Praise them? Did you think I got my just deserts? Was my eye worth what I did?"

"I had no say in it," Nate said.

"More excuses." One-Eye moved the knife above Nate's face. "Enough. It's time to take my revenge. Which eye should I cut out first? The right or the left? Or maybe I should do both at once."

Howeah of the Nemene held his war horse to a canter. He was close, very close, and he must not let the whites spot him. He had started out before sunrise and expected to soon overtake them.

It had been Nocona's idea. To send one warrior on ahead to spy on the whites. All of them wanted to do it, so Nocona plucked stems of grass and held the stems between his hands with only the ends sticking out, and each warrior had picked one.

Howeah drew the short stem.

Now here Howeah was. He looked forward to the end of the chase. To disposing of the whites and returning to his village. He missed his wife and sons. He would never admit it to his friends, but he would rather be in his lodge with his loved ones than seeking hair to hang from coup sticks.

Soon Howeah straightened and peered into the distance. His eyes, the sharpest eyes of all the Wasps, had spied something: silhouettes outlined against the horizon. Their shape left no doubt. They were horses.

Immediately, Howeah brought his own mount to a stop and swung off. His horse would stay where he left it. It was well trained. Unslinging his bow, he notched an arrow to the sinew string, crouched, and cat-footed forward.

Howeah was well versed in the deadly craft of his formidable people. As he advanced he angled to the east so that he approached the whites from out of the sun. It was not long before he saw a white man moving about. Dropping onto all fours, he crawled until he heard the man's voice raised in anger. That puzzled him. He wondered if the whites had spotted him, but there was no loud outcry or other signs of alarm.

Exercising the skill of a stalking wolf, Howeah flattened and crept nearer. He heard another voice, deeper but quieter, that reminded him of the rumble of a bear. The horses were to his left. Since the breeze was out of the north, it carried his scent away from them. The grass thinned, and he slowed. Holding the bow in front of him, he parted the blades with consummate care so they would not rustle and give him away.

Then Howeah saw them. Few times in his life had he ever been astonished. But this astonished him. For two of the white men had been stripped half naked and staked out, while the woman lay bound and unconscious.

This was new. This was different.

It interested Howeah greatly. He had never witnessed whites harm other whites. Yet plainly the skinny white with one eye intended to hurt the others. Howeah listened, wishing he spoke the white tongue, as the man with one eye railed at the others. Howeah watched, amazed, as the woman attacked the man with one eye and was brutally struck on the jaw.

Incredible happenings.

Howeah drank it in, enthralled. He found himself admiring the white with one eye. The man was like a rabid coyote.

Howeah studied the other two. The short one had been shot and the wound left untended. The big one had more muscles than any man Howeah ever saw. The man with one eye did not like the big one. The emotion that twisted one-eye's face said so.

A lot of talking took place. The man with one eye became madder. The big man on the ground was surprisingly calm. Then the man with one eye squatted and held a knife over the big one.

Howeah was riveted in fascination. He waited for the plunge of steel, the spurt of blood. But the man with one eye did not bury the blade. The man talked some more. Talked too much, in Howeah's estimation.

Howeah thought of his friends. He should get back to them so he could lead them to the whites. They would get this over with, and he could return to their village and his loved ones. But he stayed where he was, intrigued to learn what the white with one eye would do next.

As it turned out, Howeah did not have long to wait, and it was not what he expected, not what he expected at all.

"What did you say?"

"There is a Comanche behind you," Nate King whispered in case the watching warrior understood English.

One-Eye Jackson laughed and could not stop. He laughed so hard, he had to hold his side. When his mirth subsided and he could finally speak, he sputtered, "That was feeble, mister. As old as the hills. A line my grandpa might have used in his day."

"I'm telling the truth."

"You're stalling, is what you are doing," One-Eye declared. "But I'm not a yack like your friend, yonder."

"I don't know how long he's been there," Nate said. "He's watching you, and he has a bow."

One-Eye's smirk faded and his good eye narrowed. "It won't work. You must know how I feel about redskins. But I refuse to fall for it."

"Straight tongue," Nate said. "I swear by the lives of my wife and children." Jackson was right in one respect; he was grasping at a straw, but it was a real straw. Nate had seen the barest of movement in the grass, movement so slight that he almost did not notice it. The Comanche's painted face was almost invisible, but it was there.

"You'd swear by your family?" One-Eye swallowed and lowered his knife.

"Damn me if I'm not starting to believe you."

Shipley Beecher chose that moment to demand, "What are you two whispering about? What the hell is going on?"

Without saying a word, Jackson stood, walked over to the farmer, and stomped on his stomach. Beecher howled and bucked against the ropes and then lay fiercely cursing his tormentor.

One-Eye stood there, one leg slightly to one side, seemingly staring down at Beecher. When the farmer finally ran out of swearwords, Jackson stomped on him again, then came over and squatted beside Nate.

"I'll be damned."

"You saw the Comanche?"

"It took some doing but I saw him, yes." One-Eye gnawed on his lower lip. "This changes things."

"Cut us loose. We'll help you."

One-Eye shook his head. "I have a better idea. And you have only yourself to blame."

"You wouldn't," Nate said.

"That night the Shoshones did this to me," One-Eye said, touching his eye patch, "changed me. I hate redskins almost as much as I hate you. I'm also, I admit, a bit skittish about them ever getting their hands on me again."

Out of the corner of his eye, Nate watched the face in the grass. It had not moved. The warrior did not suspect he had been discovered.

"Where there is one Comanche, there are bound to be more," One-Eye said. "A lot more. There could be ten, there could be twenty. More than the three of us can handle."

"We stand a better chance together," Nate argued.

"We don't stand a chance in hell," One-Eye said. "Not against Comanches. And we both know what they will do if they get their hands on us."

Nate would rather not think about it. Comanches were notorious for torturing captives, particularly whites, especially men.

"No, sir," One-Eye said, more to himself. "The notion of them carving on me rattles me down to the bone. They might be surrounding us even as we chat, if they haven't already." He gave a slight start. "And here I am, wasting breath on you."

"I don't want to die this way," Nate said.

"I didn't want to lose an eye, either, but look at me now," One-Eye said angrily. Then, surprisingly, he smiled. "In a way, this is perfect. You'll get to feel exactly like I felt that night. You'll get to experience everything I experienced, and more. The pain. The fear. All of it."

"At least take the woman."

One-Eye shook his head. "If I throw her over a horse, the Comanches will guess what I'm up to." He shrugged. "Maybe she'll be lucky. Maybe they won't kill her. She'll wish they had after she's been some buck's squaw for a few years. But she'll be breathing."

"Don't," Nate said.

"They'll wring the spunk out of her. They'll maim her spirit and her body. She'll never be the same. Just like I never was."

"Isn't there a shred of decency left in you?"

"Save your breath. Nothing you can say will change my mind." One-Eye frowned. "I wanted to do you myself. But the Comanches will do it better. I've heard a man can last for days, in pain the whole while. That's what I call fitting."

"Congratulations," Nate said wryly. "You've sunk as low as a man can sink."

"That's what you think. Anything you want me to tell your wife when I see her?"

Nate fought down new fear. "You can tell my son to kill you slow."

"Your son?" One-Eye cocked his head. "Oh. That's right. I'd forgotten about him. Stalking Coyote, isn't that his Shoshone name? Quite the killer, folks say. Just like most 'breeds."

"Quite the tracker, too," Nate said. "Him and Shakespeare McNair."

"McNair? What does that old coot have to do with anything?"

"We've been partners for years. He's my best friend, and my neighbor, and he hasn't lost an ounce of vitality."

"You don't say?" Gnawing on his lower lip was becoming a habit for One-Eye. "There's another gent I'd rather not tangle with. Did you know the Indians all call him Carcajou? That's French for wolverine. In his younger days he was supposed to be a holy terror when his dander was up."

"He still is."

One-Eye smiled. "I know what you're up to. And it worked. I'm not fool enough to go up against your son and McNair, both. Your wife is safe."

Nate tried hard not to show the relief that coursed through him.

"But you're not," One-Eye gloated. His gaze darted right and left. "No sign of any other Comanches yet. Any last words before I ago?"

Nate merely stared.

"No? Well, I have a few. You won't want to hear them, but that will make it all the sweeter."

"Just go."

"You're being petty. One of my eyes is worth a minute of your time, don't you think?" Jackson's tone became flinty. "No one has the right to do what you did to me. I'm sure as hell no Bible-thumper, but I know there's a line in there some-where about judge not, lest ye be judged. That's what you did. You judged me, you son of a bitch, and sicced those kin of yours on me."

"There's also a line in the Bible about an eye for an eye, a tooth for a tooth."

"I didn't touch that brat's eyes!"

"No, you did something worse. You did something so despicable, the Shoshones could not believe it. You're lucky. Touch The Clouds did not have the chance to burn you at the stake after he carved on you."

"Spoiled his fun, didn't I?" One-Eye grinned. "Well, this is it. I would love to sneak back and see how they go about it, but a man shouldn't play with fire." He cradled his rifle and turned. Moving casually so as not to give away his intention, he walked over to Cynthia and poked her. She didn't stir. Then, stepping to his horse, he pretended to rummage in a saddlebag. Suddenly he vaulted into the saddle, grabbed the reins to the other two horses and the lead rope to the packhorse, and slapped his heels. In a flurry of hooves he galloped north, cackling cheerfully. "See you in hell!"

"What is he doing?" Shipley Beecher asked.

The drum of hoofbeats gradually faded. Silence fell, complete and utter silence. In the stillness, Nate swore he could hear the beat of his heart. There were just the three of them now, bound and helpless.

The three of them, and the Comanches.

CHAPTER EIGHT

Quiet lay over the prairie. Quiet save for the whisper of the wind and the rustle of grass.

A sheen of sweat caked Nate King. Drops of sweat beaded his brow. The burning sun was partly to blame. That, and his exertions.

A quarter of an hour had gone by since One-Eye Jackson fled. Nate had spent every second straining against the ropes that bound his wrists and ankles. The ropes dug into his flesh, dug deep, drawing blood. But that did not stop Nate from twisting and wrenching even as he surged upward, every muscle in his shoulders and arms bulging.

They did not have much time. The face had disappeared. The Comanche who had been spying on them had gone to fetch others, was Nate's guess.

His wrists and shoulders ached abominably, but he tried again. He heaved his big frame off the ground and tugged with all his might, then sank back, momentarily spent.

"King?" Shipley Beecher said.

Girding himself, Nate flexed his fingers.

"King! I know you can hear me."

"What do you want?"

"Where did Jackson go? Why did he race off like that? What was all that whispering about?"

"Try to break free," Nate said. "We don't have much time."

"He's coming back? Then why did he take all the horses? Even the packhorse?" Shipley paused. "As for getting loose, I wouldn't count on it, not with this bullet hole in my shoulder. I've lost a lot of blood. I'm weak and dizzy."

"You'll be dead if we don't get free." Nate tried again, calling on all the strength he possessed. The stake to which his right wrist had been tied moved ever so slightly.

"I want to ask you something," Shipley said.

"Not now."

"It's about Jackson. What did he do that made the Shoshones cut out his eye? What was so terrible?"

"He was living with a woman named Little Fawn," Nate said while working his right wrist back and forth.

"I heard him say that, yes. Did he hurt her? Or maybe kill her?"

"Before Jackson took up with Little Fawn, she

had a husband, a warrior who was killed by the Blackfeet. Little Fawn and the warrior had a daughter." Nate felt the stake give a tiny bit more.

"So?"

"The daughter was ten."

"Again, so?

"The daughter was *ten*."

"You just said that."

Nate stopped tugging and twisted his head toward the farmer. "Little Fawn left the daughter alone with Jackson one afternoon."

"Once more, so what? Did he hit her or something?"

"My wife wanted to invite Little Fawn over for supper. Little Fawn was a friend of hers. I stopped by their lodge to ask her and found the girl crying under a robe. I asked the girl what was wrong. She told me."

"Told you what?"

"I went to Touch The Clouds. He took it from there." Nate resumed his assault on the loose stake.

"Will you quit speaking in riddles and get to the point? What did Jackson do that was so—" Shipley stopped, gasped, and exclaimed, "No! Not *that*? Surely not that?"

"That," Nate said. "Jackson threatened to slit the girl's throat if she told anyone. Then he went off to hunt. When he came back, the Shoshones were waiting for him."

"And this Touch The Clouds cut out his eye?"

Shipley said. "Jackson blames you and has hated you ever since. Is that how it is?"

"We might have our own eyes cut out if we don't stop jabbering and work on these ropes." Nate arched his body. The pain in his arms and legs was excruciating, but he grit his teeth and surged upward again.

"But Jackson left like a bat out of hell."

"It's not him you have to worry about. It's Comanches," Nate explained. "A war party. They'll be here any minute." Blood was dripping from both wrists. He had loosened the right stake a little more, but it was nowhere near enough. It would take him an hour, at least. An hour they did not have. The Comanches could not be that far off.

Then Cynthia Beecher groaned and slowly sat up. Apparently forgetting her wrists were tied, she tried to move her arms. "Where is he?" she asked, and moved her jaw from side to side. "Where did that awful man who slugged me get to?"

"We have worse trouble," Nate said, and told her about the Comanches.

Sliding her legs under her, Cynthia stood. She swayed, took a step, swayed some more. "I can't clear my head," she said, and shook it. Grimacing, she moved determinedly toward them.

"Thank God!" Shipley declared.

Cynthia came to Nate, and stopped. She sank next to the stake that held his right arm, turned her back to it, and began prying at the knots. She had to look over her shoulder to see what she was doing.

Shipley was flabbergasted. "You're helping him before you help me? Does this mean all those terrible things Jackson said were true?"

"It means he was closer to me and he can free you a lot faster than I can, and that's all it means," Cynthia said testily.

"But I'm your husband, Cyn."

"Don't start, Ship. For God's sake, don't start in on me again. I need to concentrate."

The seconds became centuries, the minutes eternities. Nate lay still in order not to jiggle the rope. Cynthia pried and tugged and pulled, working feverishly. She broke a fingernail. She broke two. A finger began bleeding but she did not stop. Finally one of the knots came undone. The second proved easier.

Nate wasted no time. The moment his right wrist was free, he freed his left, then untied his ankles. He untied Cynthia, then hurried to Shipley and soon had the farmer free, as well.

"What now?" Cynthia asked, anxiously scanning the prairie. "What chance do we have against a Comanche war party?"

"We're unarmed and on foot," Shipley said. "We don't stand any chance at all."

Nate bent and pulled on one of the stakes. It took some doing but he got it out of the ground and brushed off the dirt.

"What good is that thing?" Shipley wanted to know.

"We need a weapon and it has a point," Nate said. Not much of a point, but it was better than nothing. He immediately headed west, walking briskly, forcing the others to hasten to keep up with him.

"Not so fast," Shipley Beecher complained. "My shoulder is throbbing and I can hardly walk."

"It's root hog or die," Nate said. "I can't carry you. We wouldn't get far before the Comanches caught us. You'll have to keep up."

"That's harsh, King," Shipley said. "I'm white, like you. You can't just go off and leave me." He blinked, glanced at Cynthia, and flushed red. "Or maybe you have a secret reason to want me dead."

Nate did not dignify the question with an answer. He hiked on, casting repeated glances to the south and east. The Comanches, he figured, would come from either one direction or the other. The warrior in the grass had been to the east; Comanche territory was to the south.

"Did you hear me?" Shipley demanded.

The veneer of patience Nate had clung to snapped. Whirling, he towered over the farmer, his big fists clenched. "For the last time. Nothing happened between your wife and me. Nothing *will* happen between your wife and me." He walked on before he did something both of them would regret.

Cynthia fell behind and stayed at her husband's side. She tried twice to talk to him, but he refused to reply.

Nate would be glad when he was shed of them. But right now he had a more important problem. On horseback, the war party would rapidly overhaul them. They were as good as dead unless he could pull a miracle out of his pocket, and his pockets were empty.

The unexpected delayed Howeah.

He was racing back to bring the others when he spied a riderless horse to the southwest. Since horses were as valuable to the Nemene as the yellow ore that glittered was prized by whites, he slowed to observe the animal and determine whether it was worth his attention.

A tingle ran through him. Seldom had Howeah seen so magnificent a horse.

It was a bay. Everything about it spoke of endurance and speed. One look, and he had to have it. He reined toward it, only to have it turn and trot away. He rode faster. The bay went faster. He galloped as swiftly as a raven on the wind. The bay galloped even more swiftly.

Stubbornly, Howeah kept after it. The whites who had been staked out were not going anywhere. He could spare the time needed to catch the bay and claim it as his own. It was not a wild horse. The saddle on its back told him that. A white saddle, too. Which made stealing it all the sweeter. Next to killing a white, the Nemene most loved to steal a white's horse.

But catching the bay proved to be more difficult than Howeah counted on. He had been at it awhile when he slowed and turned his mount to the south to rejoin his companions. He had traveled a short way when he glanced back and was stupefied to see the bay following him.

Howeah was not like Sargento. He did not see omens in everything. But this was a good sign. He slowed, thinking the bay might come closer, but it slowed, too, keeping the same distance between them.

"Clever," Howeah said aloud. "But I can be clever too. Keep following me and you will find out how clever."

The others were waiting for news.

"What has taken you so long?" Nocona demanded. "Did you find the whites or not?"

"We thought perhaps the whites had caught you and we were about to come look for you," Soko said.

"Are there three white men and one white woman as we thought?" Pahkah asked.

"Do the men have hair?" Sargento spoke up. Bald enemies were a peeve of his.

"I found the whites and they all have hair." Howeah shifted and pointed. "I also found that."

Their love of horseflesh was evinced in their praise of the bay, which had stopped some distance off and was staring at them.

"Why have you not caught it?" Sargento asked.

Howeah rejoined, "Who can catch the wind?"

Soko shielded his eyes from the sun to better study the animal. "It is that fast?"

"I have never seen faster," Howeah admitted. "Not even the horse of Tabbaquena."

That impressed them. Tabbaquena was a warrior of great renown among the Nemene and an acknowledged *parabio*, or leader. He was wise and without fear. He also owned more horses than any living Nemene, a herd so fabulous it was the talk of every band and the envy of every warrior. One of his horses was of such superior stock it had never been beaten in a race.

"I claim the bay for my own," Howeah declared. "But I cannot catch him on my own."

Sargento's features clouded. "You ask us to chase a horse when there are whites to slay?"

"Two of the white men are staked to the ground. The woman is tied," Howeah related.

"You have been busy," Nocona said. "Why did you not wait for us?"

More time went by as Howeah told them about the one-eyed white who had staked out the others and hit the woman and then rode off with their horses.

"The strangeness of the whites is without end," Soko said.

"They are stupid, like goats," Sargento declared.

"It is more than that," Soko said. "I believe they are born strange. They come into the world not knowing who they are or why they are here. They live their whole lives without regard for the Everywhere Spirit. Their warriors fight for pieces of metal, not to show their courage. They do not give of their bounty to one another but hoard it for themselves. No one can argue this is strange. No one can argue they live this strangeness from the cradleboard to the grave."

"As always Soko is wise," Nocona said. "Now I will try to be equally as wise. It is right we help Howeah. He has often helped each of us."

"But the whites!" Sargento protested.

"You will go to where they are staked out," Nocona said. "We will join you when we have caught the bay."

Sargento beamed, for him a rare emotion. "I will watch over them until you come. You need not hurry."

"Since Pahkah does not have a horse, let him ride with you," Nocona proposed, and Sargento's smile faded. To Pahkah, Nocona said, "Keep the whites alive. Do not harm them."

"It will be as you wish," Pahkah said.

Sargento was glowering at the world again. "I have never been fond of prairie dogs," he muttered.

The five Wasps separated, Nocona and Soko and Howeah readying their ropes as they spread out to give chase to the bay, Sargento riding north with Pahkah behind him. Of all of them, only Sargento appeared unhappy.

"Howeah always has luck," Pahkah said. "I am without a horse, yet he saw the bay first."

"I have never been fond of bays," Sargento said. His own warhorse was a pinto, as were Nocona's and Soko's mounts. The Nemene preferred pintos and paints above all others.

"Are you fond of white women? The one I saw has hair the color of straw. For a white she is appealing."

"I like to beat them," Sargento said. "They are not good for much except to use as dogs." Which was the Nemene way of saying "as beasts of burden."

"You would never take one for a wife?"

Sargento grunted. "I have four wives already. What need have I of more? Especially a useless white woman."

"Penateka took a white wife. He described her as a she-cat under the robes at night. She liked to scratch his back and make a lot of noise."

"I am not fond of noisy women. I like my women to stay quiet so I can think while we are making love," Sargento said.

"That is interesting. Myself, I do not like a lot of noise but neither do I like them to lie there like lumps of clay. A little noise and a few scratches and I am content."

"If it were not for giving us babies, and cooking our food, our own females would be almost as useless as white women."

"I am your friend. I will forget you said that. It would be well if you forget you said that, too."

"Why? I have told my wives the same thing."

"That is interesting, too. I remember you telling me once that your wives are poor cooks and do not please you much at night."

"So?"

"All four of them?"

"Yes. I have no luck when it comes to picking women."

"It is a mystery," Pahkah said.

Howeah had told them in which direction and how far to ride. They did exactly as he had said, and when they were where the staked-out whites should be, there were no whites tied to stakes.

"He told us wrong," Sargento growled.

"We must be near," Pahkah said. "Ride in circles. Make each circle larger. We are sure to find them."

Sargento complied. They were on their sixth circle when Sargento reined up and spat, "This is pointless."

"Let us think it over," Pahkah said, and did so out loud. "We know that Howeah saw the whites. He always speaks with a straight tongue. We know that we are in the area where he saw them. Since we cannot find them, they are no longer here. Perhaps they have run away."

"Someone freed them?"

"Or they freed themselves."

"We should have found the stakes, then."

"Not if the stakes were driven all the way into the earth. Only the tops would show, if that. We might have missed them."

"What do you propose?"

"We dismount and search on foot for tracks or other sign."

That is what they did. They searched and searched as the sun climbed the sky, and they were still searching when three riders appeared to the southwest. Pahkah shouted and waved his arms, and soon Nocono, Soko, and Howeah arrived, their mounts lathered with sweat.

"Where is the bay?" Sargento asked.

Howeah's expression was that of someone who had swallowed a bone by mistake. "Never mention the bay to me again."

"We could not catch him," Nocona said. "We tried trick after trick and he eluded us. He is a horse like few others."

"Did you chase him in relays?" Pahkah asked.

"Of course," Nocona said. "But our horses tired, not him." He said it with great admiration.

"I would give anything to own such an animal," Soko said.

Sargento made a slashing gesture. "You have wasted half the day and so have we." He glared at Howeah. "Those whites of yours have turned into birds and flown off into the sky."

"You cannot find them?" Howeah asked in mild surprise.

"You have eyes. Do you see them anywhere?"

Sargento retorted unkindly. "We have lost them because of your bay you could not catch."

"Do not take offense," Pahkah said to Howeah. "He was looking forward to torturing them."

"We all were," Soko said. "It is no excuse for being rude."

"I will look for them," Howeah said. "I know right where they are." He rose on his horse and scanned the prairie and then remarked, "The grass is the same everywhere you look."

"Who would have thought it?" Sargento said.

"We can find them," Howeah insisted, and kneed his mount.

Nocono suggested the rest of them spread out and scour the vicinity. They scoured, and scoured some more, and as the sun came to rest on the west rim of the world, they came together and gazed at one another in defeat. They could find no sign of where the whites had been.

"This is embarrassing," Sargento grumbled. "We find whites and then we lose them. We will be laughed at when we return to our village."

"Not if we tell no one," Pahkah said.

Nocona was watching the horizon swallow the sun. "It will be night soon. We will hunt for our supper, make camp, and rest. In the morning we will look for the whites again."

"Even if we cannot find their camp, we will ride to the northwest," Soko proposed.

"Why that direction and no other?" Sargento asked.

"The whites would not head south. That is Nemene territory. They would not go east. There is nothing but prairie. The same to the west. But to the north is the fort the whites call Bent's. It is the only place they can go for help."

"I respect your wisdom, as always," Nocona said.

They did not find any game. They had to go hungry. They had no wood for a fire, so they had to settle for a cold camp. They stayed up late, talking about coup they had counted, and family and friends. Soon after they had fallen asleep, coyotes strayed near and took to yipping and yapping and generally making it hard for everyone except old Soko to go on sleeping.

"I have never been fond of coyotes," Sargento growled. "Why do they pester us? They should be off filling their bellies."

"If they tasted better I would kill one for my own belly," Pahkah said.

"They are too much like dogs," Nocona said.

The Nemene never ate dog meat. To them, it was the same as eating one's cousin. Some of the neighboring tribes engaged in the revolting practice, which did not endear them to the Nemene.

"I will go throw clods of dirt at them," Sargento announced, and walked off into the night.

"He is in one of his moods," Nocona said.

"I do not blame him," Pahkah responded. "If I had moods, I would be in one too."

The coyotes were still yipping. Then one

yipped louder and sharper than the rest, and silence claimed the plain.

Sargento came out of the dark and reclaimed his spot. "We can sleep the rest of the night in peace."

Unfortunately, most of them had trouble falling off again. They had too much on their minds.

The sun broke on four tired warriors and one somewhat older warrior who was fully refreshed.

Stretching and smiling, Soko said, "I am ready to renew our hunt. How about the rest of you?"

"If you were a coyote I would beat you to death," Sargento said.

They climbed on their warhorses and set out and had gone perhaps the distance a turtle can crawl in half a day when Howeah whooped and indicated the ground to one side. "The stakes!"

"We were this close and did not know it?" Pahkah said in disgust.

"The important thing is we can track them now," Sargento said. "We can track them and we can kill them."

CHAPTER NINE

Nate King had a newfound faith in miracles. There had been no sign of the Comanches. Not the day before. Not during the night.

Now, the morning sun an hour into its celestial flight, Nate was hiking west. The Beechers were on each side of him. They were not speaking to one another. A heated spat the evening before was to blame. They had gone off a short way so he would not hear. But they became so mad, and raised their voices so loud, he could not help but overhear. The thrust of their fight had been all too apparent: him.

Shipley was as green as the grass, figuratively speaking. Cynthia had protested her innocence with vigor, but her husband refused to accept her word that nothing had happened.

Nate had not spoken a word to her all morning.

Deliberately. Several times he caught Shipley glaring at him, but Shipley always looked away when Nate caught him.

Squabbling spouses was an aggravation Nate did not need. He had more than enough to deal with, namely, no horses, no food, no water, virtually no weapons, he and the farmer were only half clothed, and a Comanche war party was after them.

"Why are you leading us west?" Shipley Beecher abruptly broke his long silence. "Isn't Bent's Fort north of us?"

"Yes," Nate confirmed. "But the Comanches will expect us to make straight for it. By going west and swinging north later we can throw them off our scent."

"It will take longer this way, won't it?" Shipley asked.

"Longer but safer," Nate said.

"We could be going to all this bother for nothing," Shipley groused. "It could be the Comanches aren't even after us."

"Could be, but I wouldn't count on it."

"What if my wife and I want to reach the post as quickly as we can? What if we were to head north now instead of continuing west? Would you try to stop us?"

"You are grown adults," Nate answered. "You're free to do however you please. But for your wife's sake, I hope you don't." He knew it was a mistake the instant he said it, but the harm had been done.

"Rub my nose in it, why don't you?" Shipley snapped. "Jackson was right about you."

"Don't start that nonsense again," Nate warned.

"How does it feel, knowing you have destroyed a marriage?" the farmer spat.

"What?"

"What?" Cynthia echoed, startled. She had been walking with her head hung low, a portrait of misery. "How was that again?"

"A divorce," Shipley said.

The color drained from Cynthia. She broke stride but recovered. "You're not serious, Ship. Not after three years together. Not over a trifle."

"One person's trifle is another's mountain," Shipley responded. "I don't take what you did lightly. I don't take it lightly at all."

"How can you accept the word of a man like Jackson over the word of your wife?" Cynthia asked in the fragile manner of someone whose heart was being crushed. "I made a sacred vow to be true to you."

To that Shipley had no reply.

Nate was at a loss. He had not done anything wrong. But the farmer refused to believe it. Shipley had made up his mind the unspeakable had happened and would not accept any argument to the contrary. How was Nate to convince him?

What would it take to batter down the closed door of Shipley's mind to admit the light of reason?

Cynthia compounded matters by saying, "I'm beginning to wonder if you ever truly loved me. How else can you think of casting me aside so lightly?"

Shipley suddenly stopped and faced her. "So you claim you still love me, is that it?"

"I never stopped."

"Prove it. I am heading for Bent's Fort. You can come with me or you can stay with the mountain man. But if you stay, we get a divorce. It's your choice. Which will it be?"

Nate had a choice of his own to make. Keep quiet, or try to save them from their folly. "It's best if we stick together. The Comanches are out there somewhere."

"So you keep saying," Ship said. "But I've seen through your excuse to keep my wife by your side. Head west if you want. But you'll do it without me." He looked at Cynthia. "Which way are *you* heading?"

There it was. Impaled on her honor. Nate had to say nothing, knowing what she would do and knowing it was the worst decision of her life.

Sadness etched Cynthia's pretty face, sadness so deep and profound it was heart-wrenching. "I married you for better or worse."

Shipley Beecher puffed up like a bantam rooster. He took her hand and looked at Nate as if to say *See? I've won!*

"You're making a mistake," Nate tried.

"If so, it is *ours* to make." Shipley led his wife to the north, saying condescendingly, "Come, my dear. We can make it to Bent's Fort without him."

Cynthia moved like someone sleepwalking.

Nate watched until they were specks. Then he wheeled to the west and strode with long, angry strides. But he only went about a hundred yards. Then he stopped and sighed and said, "Damn."

Turning, Nate hurried north.

Most easterners envisioned the prairie as mile after mile of endless flat. Major Stephen Long, John Charles Fremont, and Colonel Stephen Kearney had all crisscrossed the Great Plains and given accounts of their discoveries, accounts that were widely circulated, and all three made note of the endless miles of flat.

But the truth was not the same as the perception. For while the prairie was essentially flat, it was split by washes and gullies and hollows and, on occasion, by canyons and low hills.

Cynthia sighted the hills first. She was plodding along, in the grip of despair, when she looked up, and there they were. Bumps, at first, which bulged into low hills sprinkled with vegetation other than grass. "Look yonder."

Shipley had his head down and was listlessly massaging his wounded shoulder. "Eh?" He stopped. "I'll be switched! I'll bet there's water. My throat is so dry I could drink a lake."

"We must be careful," Cynthia cautioned. "If there is water, there are more likely to be wild animals or hostiles."

"The only hostile we need worry about is Nate King," Shipley said. "He's lived with Injuns for so long he's forgotten how to be white."

"I would rather we not talk about him."

The buffalo grass crackled under their weary tread. Here and there were tumbleweeds. Random points of yellow became sunflowers. Clover and daisies sprinkled the rising ground. A few oaks and sycamores dotted the slopes.

"There has to be water. There just has to." Shipley ran his dry tongue over his equally dry lips.

A lark took wing from out of the clover. Farther on, a thicket disgorged a bevy of quail.

"This would be a good spot for a farm," Shipley said. "Provided there is enough water."

Cynthia stared at him, her sadness deepening, and ran her tongue over her own lips. "Yes, it would."

"We'll mention it to Hiram and Elmer when we meet up with them."

The first hill would not have taxed a kitten, but it taxed them. When they reached the top they stopped and bent over with their hands on their knees and sucked air into their lungs.

The next hill was greener. The hill after that the greenest yet. On the far side lay the most welcome sight in the world, a blue oval that covered a third of an acre.

Shipley rubbed his eyes and blurted, "Tell me I'm seeing things! Tell me it's not there!"

"It seems to be," Cynthia said.

"It can't be a mirage if we both see it." Shipley lurched down the slope, gaining speed as he went. At the bottom he tried to stop, but he was moving too fast and his legs were too weak. He squawked as he pitched headlong into the water. Shaking himself, he sat up. The level only came as high as his chest. Giddy with delight, he splashed water on himself and then on Cynthia when she wearily sank down, her legs under her, and dipped a palm.

"We should stay here a week and rest," Shipley happily proposed.

Cynthia sipped delicately from her hand, then moistened her cheeks and brow. "What would we do for food?"

"I'm sure I can kill us something." Shipley ducked under and resurfaced. He went under again and stayed under for as long as he could hold his breath. Then, laughing, he drank greedily, waded out, and collapsed on his back. "If I drink any more I'll be sick."

Trees shaded half the pond. Brush overgrew the rest. Animal tracks were everywhere.

"Our own Garden of Eden," Shipley said, gazing about. "It could not be more perfect." He closed his eyes.

Cynthia dipped her hand in again. "The Garden had a serpent. We would do well to remember that."

"Our serpent is Nate King. I wonder if he knows this is here."

"I wonder if the Comanches do," Cynthia said. She tilted her palm and let wonderfully cool water fill her mouth and trickle down her chin and neck. For the first time in days she smiled. "Maybe you're right. Maybe everything will turn out fine." She bent to dip her hand a third time. The reflections that stared back at her forced a bleat of fear from her throat. "Run!" she cried, and rose to do so but iron fingers closed on her arms.

Shipley's eyes snapped open. He started to rise. "Unhand her!" he bellowed, and received the blunt end of a lance in the ribs. Clutching his side, he rolled about in agony and hissed through clenched teeth.

"This one is weak," Sargento said, hefting his lance. "He will scream when we cut him."

Pahkah and Howeah were studying the woman they held.

"I like her hair," the latter said. "It gleams like the yellow metal whites love so much."

"She is tiny," Pahkah said. "Her nose is like a ferret's and her teeth are like a badger's."

Nocona had stood to one side, ready to loose a shaft if the man or the woman sought to flee. Cupping a hand to his mouth, he shouted, "We have them, Soko. Bring the horses."

From out of the thick brush on the other side came the older warrior, leading their mounts.

"Oh God, oh God, oh God." Shipley gaped in horror. "These must be the Comanches Nate King warned us about!"

"Be brave," Cynthia said, looking from one warrior to the other. In only one painted face was there any hint of friendliness.

"Be brave?" Shipley uttered a shrill laugh that ended in a gurgle of raw panic. "Don't you understand? We are as good as dead."

Sargento could only take so much whining and trembling. He struck out with the blunt end of the lance at the white man's temple, stunning him. "First I will cut out his tongue."

"The woman shows courage," Pahkah said.

"Yes, she does," Howeah agreed. "She reminds me of a golden eagle, this one. Look at how she holds her head, high and proud."

Sargento glanced over sharply. "She is all of ours. Not yours. Remember that if you are thinking what I think you are thinking."

"It might prove interesting to tame this golden eagle," Howeah said.

"Faugh!" Sargento signaled his disapproval. "Talk to this elk in rut, Nocona. The white woman is not his. She belongs to all of us."

"There are no spoils to share," Pahkah said. "They have no horses, no weapons. Her dress is too small for any of my women."

Howeah touched the woman's hair and she did not flinch. "It is a fitting name. I will call her Golden Eagle."

"Are your ears plugged with wax?" Sargento asked.

Cynthia stood quietly, smothering her fear through force of will. She had never been so afraid in her life, but she knew she must not show it. She listened closely to what her captors were saying. Not that she could understand it. To her, the Comanche tongue was so much gibberish. But their tone, their inflection, indicated how they might feel about her.

"You want this woman?" Nocona asked Howeah.

"The idea appeals to me, brother."

"Our father might approve, but our mother will not. Your other wives will not, either."

Sargento was growing angry. "Put an end to this talk of keeping her. Nocona led this war party but we have a say. And I say both the man and the woman should die."

"Perhaps a trade can be struck," Pahkah suggested. "Howeah keeps the woman if he agrees to give each of us a horse."

"Four horses for a white woman is too many," Sargento scoffed. "Why give so much for something so worthless?"

Cynthia thought she had a fair understanding of their sentiments. The dark one hated her. The handsome one liked her. The tall one seemed to take the handsome one's side. The one with the crooked nose was neutral. A slightly older warrior was coming toward them leading horses and so far had not taken part.

"I decide what has worth to me and what does not," Howeah said.

"It is wrong of Nocona to take sides," Sargento said. "He must treat us all fairly."

Suddenly Shipley Beecher leaped to his feet and bolted. He had recovered and had been listening to their guttural jabber. Whatever they were arguing about, they had forgotten about him, which suited him fine. But they might remember him any moment, and bind him. He could not let that happen. Once he was tied up, he was a goner. So he gambled, pushed to his feet, and ran for his life.

"What does he think he is doing?" Pahkah asked.

"He is trying to escape," Nocona guessed.

"On foot? When we have horses?" Howeah marveled. "How far does he think he will get?"

"Not far," Sargento said. "He runs like my sister, and she is as slow as tree sap." He threw back his arm to cast his lance.

"Hold," Nocona said. "A lance wound sometimes kills even when we do not want it to." He gestured. "You bring him down, brother."

Howeah calmly raised his bow and sighted along the arrow. At the *twang* of the sinew string, the shaft streaked true to its target.

Pain seared Shipley's left thigh. Stumbling, he

grabbed at his leg and tore his hand on the barbed tip of the arrow. He tried to keep running but his leg would not cooperate. The upshot was that he went another five yards and pitched to his face. Frantic, he gripped the arrow and sought to snap the tip off so he could pull the arrow out and keep going. But he was weaker than he figured. The best he could do was bend the arrow slightly.

"He is about as strong as my sister, too," Sargento said.

Pahkah took the other side, and together they half carried, half dragged their captive and shoved him flat on his belly.

Shipley howled in torment. He grabbed at his leg and accidentally jarred the arrow, which compounded the pain tenfold. He bit his lower lip to stifle another outcry, bit it so hard, blood flowed. He stifled the outcry but he did whimper.

"He is worse than my dog," Pahkah muttered.

Of the five Wasps only Soko had a war club. He stepped up behind their captive and rapped him over the back of the head. He did not strike to kill or maim, but to render the white man unconscious.

"At last he is quiet," Sargento said.

The Nemene made camp. Each of them saw to his own horse. Pahkah gathered firewood. Soko kindled a fire. Nocona and Sargento went off to hunt. That left Howeah to guard the whites.

Cynthia Beecher wanted to tend Shipley, but she was unsure how the Comanches would react. She decided to find out. She took a tentative step toward him, watching the handsome Comanche for a sign of anger. When he did not do anything, she took another, longer step. Then she was on her knees, rolling Shipley over. He had a bump and a gash on his temple from where he had been struck by the lance. The blow from the war club, surprisingly, had not broken the scalp. The worst wound was the one in his thigh. Thankfully, it was not bleeding much.

Cynthia wanted to take the arrow out. She gripped it near the feathers, intending to break it.

Howeah pushed her. He did not push her roughly but it was sufficient to cause her to fall on her side.

Fearing she was about to be attacked, Cynthia flung her arms protectively over her head and face. When the attack did not materialize, she looked up at the handsome Comanche. "Why?" she asked, knowing he could not understand her, but desperate to understand herself. "Why won't you let me take the arrow out?"

Howeah tilted his head. Her sounds were so many bird chirps to him, but he had some idea of what she was saying. She was upset because he had not let her break the arrow. But fashioning arrows required much time, much effort. Warriors always took special care of them. They did not use one unless they were sure of hitting what they wanted to hit. Afterward, whenever possible, they reclaimed the arrows to use again. To break one was a mild calamity.

Howeah slung his bow over his shoulder. Bending over the white man, he grasped the shaft with both hands, below the tip. Then, pulling slowly but forcefully, he extracted it. The arrow had not lodged against a bone so it came out with little difficulty. The feathers were wet with blood but would dry. He slid the shaft into his quiver and stepped back.

"Thank you," Cynthia said.

Her tone suggested some form of gratitude, which amused Howeah. He did not care about the white man, only about his arrow.

Pahkah returned bearing broken tree limbs. "I saw the tracks of many animals," he mentioned. "We can stay here many sleeps if we want."

Soko produced two items greatly prized by his people, a steel and flint, which he had found on a dead white two winters ago. Before the coming of the whites, starting fires had taken much time and effort. Steels and flints made it ridiculously easy.

Cynthia sat and cradled Shipley's head in her lap. She was surprised her fear was fading. She knew what the Comanches were going to do. Or thought she knew. She would spend the rest of her days in a Comanche lodge, perhaps as the wife of the handsome warrior who had taken a shine to her. Her only consolation, such as it was, was that alive was better than dead. Deep inside her crawled the hope that one day she might escape. Or that other whites would find out she was a captive and arrange a trade. It had happened before.

Nocona and Sargento carried a doe strung on a limb when they came through the trees. A small doe, not much more than a fawn, but enough meat for all.

Nocona did the butchering, Soko the cooking. The older warrior had a knack for taking a haunch from the fire when the meat was at its juicy, tastiest best. They ate with relish, their first deer meat in days, licking their fingers between pieces.

Cynthia's stomach growled, embarrassing her. The handsome warrior heard, and slicing a piece of meat from the chunk he was eating, tossed it to her. She caught it, then nearly dropped it, it was so hot and slippery with grease. Her nose wrinkled in distaste but her empty stomach overrode her nose. She was ravenous. She forced herself to eat slowly and savor each chew.

Toward the end of the meal Shipley groaned and opened his eyes. They were as blank as empty slates. Gradually, recognition dawned, and he said, "Cyn?"

"Stay still. The Comanches are eating."

"They have food?" Shipley sniffed, and rose on his elbows. He stared longingly at the roasting haunch. "What I wouldn't give for a bite."

Guilt spiked Cynthia. She had not saved any of her piece for him. "Let me try." She caught the handsome warrior's eye and pointed at the spit and then at her husband. The warrior motioned sharply. "I think that means no."

"Damn them!" Ship spat. "It's not enough they put an arrow in me. It's not enough they plan to torture and kill me. They can't extend the common courtesy of some food."

"Keep your voice down."

Shipley was working himself into a fit. "Savages! That's all they are! Andrew Jackson was right. They deserve to be exterminated, every last stinking one of them!"

"Hush, consarn it," Cynthia cautioned. "Or would you rather be shot with another arrow?"

Shipley grit his teeth and hissed. "If only I had a brace of pistols. I would show these devils."

"I think that one likes me," Cynthia said, pointing at the handsome warrior.

"What?"

"He's taken a shine to me, unless I miss my guess." Cynthia figured it would give Shipley a chuckle. She was mistaken.

"Dear God, woman. First the mountain man and now this smelly heathen! Is there no bottom to the depths to which you will sink?"

"How dare you!" Cynthia fumed. "And how many times must I tell you that nothing happened between Nate King and me?"

Before Shipley could answer, all five Comanches stood and surrounded them. The dark one drew his knife.

"I'm in for it now," Shipley said.

CHAPTER TEN

It sounded, on first hearing it, like the keen of the wind over rocky crags. But as Nate King listened longer, it became more the cry of an animal in the throes of agony. Longer yet, and Nate realized the wail came from human lips. His skin crawling, he glided swiftly but cautiously around the base of the next hill. A welcome splash of blue greeted him, a pond where he would never have guessed there was one.

The smell of water, after so long without, made him yearn for a taste to relieve the torment of having gone so long without. But Nate did not rush blindly forward. Not with Comanches in the vicinity. He picked his way through the thick growth bordering the pond and beheld that which he had suspected he would find but fervently hoped he would not.

Shipley Beecher had been stripped naked and staked out. This time Nate had not been there to effect an escape, and what was left of Beecher brought to mind a mule deer after the hide had been stripped but before the hunter who shot it began carving the meat. A hideous ruin of the creature it had once been.

The farmer's chest rose and fell in great, labored breaths. The flame of life that animated Beecher had burned low and would soon be extinguished.

Of the Comanches, hoofprints revealed they had ridden south toward Comanche territory.

Nate edged closer. He did not want to look but he had to. The things the Comanches had done were the sorts of things white people talked about when atrocities were mentioned. Those same white people tended to forget or overlook the undeniable historical fact that whites had their share of atrocities to their dubious credit.

Nate's stomach churned. He had to look away. He could not endure the sight of Beecher's face for more than a few seconds. The ghastly dark sockets, the cavity where the nose had been, and the awful travesty of a mouth, were sights he would never forget.

On the other side of Beecher was a pile Nate could not quite identify. Something pink and wrinkled and seeped in blood. Nate leaned over Beecher for a better view and his stomach churned anew. The pile was skin.

Swallowing bitter bile, Nate hunkered. "Shipley?" he said softly.

The travesty of a mouth moved but produced inarticulate noises.

"Shipley, it's Nate King. There is nothing I can do for you. If you understand, nod?"

The farmer's head moved.

"Did they take your wife?"

Again the skinless chin bobbed.

"They have horses and I don't," Nate said. "You know what that means, don't you?" He paused, and when Shipley nodded, he went on. "I'm sorry, truly sorry. But you brought this on yourself by being so pigheaded." Perhaps that was cruel. But it was also honest.

The flesh where Beecher's lips had been moved. The sounds, though, were not words.

"I can't understand you," Nate said. "Take your time. Speak slowly." He bent down. Close enough to see into Beecher's mouth. To see that the man no longer had a tongue. "Never mind."

Shipley lay still awhile. Then he uttered more sounds and his right hand moved.

"Do you want me to cut you loose?" Nate asked. A sharp rock would have to suffice since One-Eye Jackson had taken his bowie and tomahawk.

Shipley feebly shook his head. Again his hand moved, his finger and thumb describing the same motions.

"Are you sure?"

The chin dipped.

"I don't have a gun, remember?" Nate mentioned. "All I have is the picket stake."

Once again Shipley's finger pointed at his head and his thumb curled as if squeezing a trigger.

"It will hurt like the dickens," Nate said. A stupid thing to say, he thought, in light of the circumstances.

For the third time the finger and thumb mimicked the firing of a gun.

Palming the stake, Nate hesitated. As much as the man had annoyed him, he bore Beecher no ill will. He would rather there was a more humane way. Just then a dragonfly streaked past his head and out over the pond.

Beecher gurgled and blubbered.

"I've had a brainstorm," Nate remarked. He explained, and when he was done, the farmer nodded.

Untying the ropes took some doing. The knots were not only tight, they were slick with blood. At length Nate succeeded, and slipping his hands under Beecher's shoulders, dragged him toward the spring. At the contact of his fingers with the skinless flesh, Nate flinched.

Holding Beecher's head above the water, Nate waded out. It rose over his feet, his ankles, his shins. Soon he was waist-deep. Beecher was in up to his chest, his legs much too weak to support him.

Nate felt he should say something. "So help me

God, I never laid a finger on your wife." He was going to say Cynthia never made advances, but the words caught in his throat.

The ghastly apparition mewed.

"Folks say it's painless," Nate said. "But the people who say it wouldn't rightly know."

The dragonfly whisked within inches of Shipley Beecher and darted away again.

"I wish there was another way," Nate said. He could not put it off any longer. He let go. He stepped back until the bubbles and the ripples stopped, then groped and hauled the limp figure onto dry ground. He avoided looking at the face. The more he did, the more it would haunt him later.

Nate dragged the body a score of feet from the pond. He had nothing to dig with so he roved in search of a suitable rock or stout tree limb. Suddenly the brush crackled. Nate raised the stake, holding it as he would a knife. He feared the Comanches had doubled back, or that a grizzly had caught his scent. But when the undergrowth parted, it revealed something else entirely.

"You!" Walking over, Nate threw an arm over the bay and pressed his forehead to its neck. Nearly overcome, he couldn't speak for the lump in in his throat, not for a spell, anyhow.

Dust caked the animal's coat. Scratch marks bore mute testimony to the hardships it had been through.

While the bay drank, Nate pondered. It was too

late in the day to give chase to the war party. Night would fall within an hour, forcing him to stop. Better off, he reasoned, to wait out the night at the pond and go after them at dawn.

It was almost dark when Nate finished burying Shipley Beecher. "Ashes to ashes, dust to dust," was all Nate said.

The beaded parfleches crafted by Winona were still on the bay. From one Nate slid a folding knife he had used in his trapping days. The blade was five inches long and razor sharp. He stuck the knife in a pocket. A spare shirt was in the other parfleche. Nate shrugged into it and ran his hands over the buckskin. Unfortunately, he did not carry a spare set of moccasins. He solved that by cutting strips from a blanket and wrapping the strips around his feet.

Filling the coffeepot came next. While coffee brewed, Nate treated himself to pemmican. In his famished state he was tempted to eat every piece he had, but he limited himself to half a dozen.

It felt wonderful have a full belly. To have his horse and food. To have plenty of water. Nate lay back and contentedly patted his stomach. He still needed guns and a knife and footwear. But they were problems for the morrow.

Nate tried not to think of Cynthia in the clutches of the Comanches, tried not to think of what the Comanches might be doing to her. He figured she had witnessed the torture and hoped she could bear the horror. She had impressed him as being strong inside, certainly stronger than her husband, but some things were so unspeakably shocking, inner strength wasn't a sufficient shield.

Over the course of his years in the wilderness, Nate had witnessed many such acts. He never talked about them, never thought about them if he could help it. But now and again, in unguarded moments, they blazed up out of the depths of his memory to sear him with their violence.

The *horror*. It was the one aspect of life that most mystified him. That people were born to suffer and die seemed, on the face of it, pointless, if not cruel. Where was the purpose in a baby coming down with the croup and dying? Where the meaning in a village being wiped out by smallpox? Where the sense in what Shipley Beecher had suffered, even if he did bring it down on his own head?

The *horror*. It pervaded all existence. Every creature was subject to it, from the so-called lowest to the highest. It was part and parcel of all that was, and had been for as long as humankind could remember.

Nate once asked a missionary why bad things happened to good people. The missionary's answer? That God sent His rain to fall on the just and the unjust. Which was all well and good. But why create life only to have it die? Why fill a breast with hope and inflict the horror?

Some years ago, a Shoshone who had lived

more than ninety winters mentioned to Nate that the world made perfect sense if regarded in the right way. According to the venerable ancient, all life was born to struggle and die. Nate had agreed, and the wrinkled Shoshone went on to say that the purpose to life lay in the struggle, not the dying. The struggle, the Shoshone argued, was life's whetstone. Life's way of sharpening the spirit so that those who left the world left it stronger than when they came into it.

Nate disagreed. The baby who came down with the croup was not made stronger. The Mandans, a friendly, vital people afflicted by smallpox, were not made stronger. They were wiped out.

To Nate, the horror had no purpose. It simply was. The horror was woven into the tapestry of existence much as a thread was woven into a quilt. It could not be denied, although it could be ignored. But it need not be dwelled upon. For the horror was not the only aspect to existence. There was life itself. The sweet, heady feeling of being alive, and of experiencing all the good life offered.

It was with such thoughts running through his head that Nate eventually fell asleep. He slept like one dead and woke up, as usual, before first light. A couple of cups of coffee and several pieces of pemmican, and he headed out in pursuit.

Midmorning brought an unwelcome surprise in the form of gray clouds scuttling in from the west. By early afternoon the cloud cover stretched from horizon to horizon. The wind picked up, bringing with it the scent of moisture.

The signs were all there. Nate needed to find cover, and quickly, but there was none to be had. He was in the middle of miles of flat. There was him, and the bay, and the grass. That was it. He rode faster.

The clouds darkened. To the west flashes of light danced in their depths. Distant rumbling heralded worse to come.

Soon the wind shrieked like a banshee, whipping the grass into a frenzy. A few scattered drops of rain fell. Cold drops, one of which struck Nate's neck and trickled under his shirt.

Nate was running out of time. Suddenly he stiffened. A hint of uneven ground ahead drew him at a gallop.

It was a buffalo wallow. A depression about ten feet in circumference and about a foot deep. It reeked of buffalo urine. Bulls would urinate in the dirt, then roll in it to cake their hairy bulks with mud to ward off insects.

Nate's nose crinkled and the bay balked, but he gigged it into the wallow, slid down, and grabbed the bridle. The wind buffeted him. More cold drops fell, slashing at his face like tiny knives. He was running out of time.

Long ago Nate had taught the bay a trick. By tugging on the bridle and placing firm pressure on its front leg, he brought it down onto its side.

"Good boy," he said as the horse obeyed. "I can't afford to lose you again."

The sky was black. Nate could barely see his hand at arm's length as he lay across the bay with his cheek on its neck. "Easy now," he said, patting it. "We've been through this before."

The storm broke with a ferocious crash. From the roiling clouds gushed a deluge. Lightning split the heavens, thunder boomed.

Within seconds Nate was drenched. The drops pelted like hail. Between the rain and the wind he could hardly breathe. Covering his mouth and nose, he breathed through his fingers.

The world was a liquid roar. Except for the lightning, Nate might as well be at the bottom of a well. A bolt struck so close he swore it singed his hair. The thunder about deafened him. He felt the bay quake. Worried it would bolt, he stroked its neck and spoke soothingly in its ear, but whether it heard him over the tempest, he couldn't say.

The shriek of the wind swelled to a constant howl, as if every wolf that ever lived was joined in chorus.

Nate raised himself up to see if he could spot a break to the west and nearly had his head ripped from his neck. Lowering it again, he sucked air into his lungs. He placed a hand flat on the ground to brace himself and discovered the wallow was filling with water. Already it was a couple of inches deep. If it rose much higher the bay

would have to stand, turning it into a living lightning rod.

Yet another flash lit the prairie. In its glare Nate
saw an animal crouched at the wallow's edge. It
saw him, too, and left no doubt as to its intention
by crouching and baring its fangs.

Cynthia had withdrawn into herself. The brutal-
ity of the outer world had driven her into the
safety of the inner one. She paid no attention to
what went on around her. Her eyes were open,
but they did not see. She had ears, but they did
not hear. To her, the outer world was dead. As
dead as her husband. As dead as the man she had
wronged, and she could never forgive herself.

For as long as she lived, she would never forget
the sounds Shipley made. Those awful, terrible
sounds. He had tried to be brave. He had tried
not to scream. But the things the Comanches did
would break anyone, and poor, luckless Shipley
had broken, had become a wailing, weeping husk
of a human being.

Cynthia didn't blame him. She blamed herself.
So what if coming west had been his idea? So what
is she had argued against it? So what if he had not
heeded Nate King? She should have done something. She should have stopped him, somehow. Exactly how, she could not say. It was enough that she
blamed herself, enough that she was so wretchedly
miserable. She did not care what happened to her.

Such was her mental and emotional state the evening her captors made camp by the spring where One-Eye Jackson had first appeared. She was not aware of being lowered from a horse. She was not aware of the small fire, or when the warriors turned in to sleep, leaving one to keep watch. She sat and stared numbly into nothing and felt only nothingness inside.

Then came the moment that jarred her. That snapped her out of her inner world and into the outer. That reminded her of who she was and where she was and what was being done to her.

The catalyst was a hand on her leg. Not her hand, another's.

One instant Cynthia was staring blankly into space, the next she was staring at the handsome Comanche. He had squatted in front of her and was regarding her with a look any woman would recognize.

The handsome Comanche said something to her, and smiled, and cupped her chin. Cynthia remembered the same fingers holding a knife, the very knife that gouged out her husband's eyes. The hilt of that knife was inches from her hand, in a sheath on the warrior's hip.

The handsome Comanche was still smiling when the blade sheared into his throat. The look of astonishment that came over him was almost comical. So was the crimson that spurted from his nostrils and his mouth.

Cynthia was in motion before the handsome

Comanche toppled. Yanking the blade out, she dashed to the war horses. She had been riding double on the handsome Comanche's horse, and the animal was used to her. Which accounted for why it did not try to throw her when she vaulted onto its back and slapped her legs against its sides.

Yells and bellows followed Cynthia into the night. She did not know which direction she was fleeing; she simply rode, hoping she could vanish into the darkness before the Comanches recovered their wits and came after her. She should have known better.

Not for nothing were the Comanches the scourge of the plains.

Sargento led the pursuit. He had been the first to reach Howeah, the first to see what the white woman had done. He was the first to reach the horses and give chase. When he looked back, Nocona was kneeling beside his dead brother while Pahkah and Soko dashed to their mounts.

Sargento smiled. He would overtake the white woman before them. Which was how he wanted it to be. He had not liked having her along. He yearned to do to her as they had done to her husband.

Sargento hated the white race, hated them with an intense passion rare even for a Comanche. Were it up to him, the Nemene would exterminate every last one.

Whites had killed Sargento's father. Sargento had seen but seven winters when his father went on a raid against white settlers. The raid had been successful in that seventeen whites were slain and over fifty horses stolen. Only one warrior lost his life.

According to warriors who witnessed it, his father had snuck into a corral to steal a particularly fine horse. But the whites inside a cabin to which the corral was attached heard the milling horses. A rifle poked out a window and a slug took the top of his father's head off.

The war party recovered the body and brought it back to the village.

Sargento would never forget that day. He had stood with his hand in his mother's hand, staring into the pale, lifeless face that had once been so strong and loving, and a hatred had been born that would last as long as he lived. As soon as he was old enough, he joined every war party he could, went on every raid he could, killed every white he could. Men, women, children, their age or gender made no difference. So long as they were white, he killed them.

Now here Sargento was, about to kill another. He had lost sight of the white woman's straw-hued hair, but he was confident he would soon catch up to her. His warhorse was swifter than Howeah's. Not much swifter, it was true, but enough that the outcome was not in doubt.

Too late, Sargento realized he had lost her. She

was no longer ahead of him. Instantly, he slowed and twisted every which way, but the white woman and Howeah's warhorse had disappeared.

Sargento was mad. He had blundered. He had let his mind drift when he should have focused on her and only her. He was scouring the benighted prairie for the umpteenth time when Pahkah and Soko came up on either side of him.

"You have lost her," the older warrior said. A statement, not a question.

Sargento scowled.

"How could you?" Pahkah criticized. "She is white and a woman, yet you let her elude you?"

"Her horse is a Nemene horse," Sargento said.

"We cannot track her without torches," Soko said. "But there is no need. She will head for Bent's Fort. We can give chase at dawn and will again have her our captive by sunset."

"Captive?" Sargento spat. "She slew Howeah. For that she dies. She dies as her man died."

"I have never liked cutting women," Soko said.

Sargento grunted. "I can cut anyone, anytime. Leave her to me if the rest of you are squeamish."

They found Nocona preparing to take the body south.

"Wait until morning and one of us will go with you," Pahkah suggested.

"It is better to ride in the cool of the night," Nocona said. "I will go alone. He was my brother. The rest of you find the white woman and do what we should have done when we caught her. It was foolish of my brother to want her for a wife, foolish of me not to dispute him."

"You can depend on me, my friend," Sargento said. "The white woman will die a hundred deaths for your brother."

Sargento, Pahkah, and Soko listened to the *clomp* of hooves until Nocona had faded into the night.

"Now there are three," Soko said.

"More than enough for one white woman," Sargento declared. He sat cross-legged by the fire, took a whetstone from his pouch, and honed his knife. He honed it long after the other two fell asleep, all the while thinking of the many ways to kill slowly yet with the utmost pain. The woman had a lot to answer for. For Howeah. For Sargento's father. For being white.

Dawn was crisp and clear but it did not stay clear. Clouds blanketed the blue, and by noon a storm was imminent.

"The rain will delay us," Pahkah said.

"It will not delay me," Sargento asserted, but his boast was thrown back in his face by nature's tantrum. The whipping wind, the pelting rain forced them to seek shelter in a gully and wait out the worst of it.

There was one consolation. The storm would slow the white woman, too.

The rain ended about the middle of the afternoon. The three warriors had been under way only briefly when Soho raised an arm and pointed.

Outlined against the gradually brightening sky to the northwest was the unmistakable silhouette of a horse and rider. The rider had hair the color of straw.

"She has not seen us yet," Pahkah said.

"I say we follow and take her after the sun has set and she has stopped for the night," Soko proposed.

"You can wait if you want," Sargento said, digging his heels into his mount.

Pahkah and Soko looked at one another.

"We cannot let his knife do all the cutting," Pahkah said.

"I agree," Soko replied.

The Wasps swept toward their prey.

CHAPTER ELEVEN

Nate King drew the folding knife from his pocket. He opened the blade and raised it to strike at the creature crouched on the wallow's rim. But the next bolt of lightning revealed what it was: a coyote that whirled and raced into the maelstrom.

Nate laughed out loud but could not hear his laughter for the crashing thunder and the whiplash wind. The bay raised its head. The rising water would soon force them to leave the wallow whether Nate wanted to or not. He decided to wait as long as possible. Once they were in the open, they risked a bolt from above.

Not a minute later the rain slackened, the wind dropped, the lighting seared the sky with less and less frequency.

Within ten minutes the storm had rumbled on

into the distance, leaving a sodden prairie and cool air in its wake.

Nate resumed the chase. His buckskins were soaked, but he didn't bother to take them off and wring them out. He had been soaked before. A little wet never hurt anyone. And he had lost time to make up.

The storm had driven all the birds from the sky and all the animals into their burrows, dens, and lairs. Nary a prairie dog stirred. Nate had the plain to himself.

All traces of the war party had been obliterated. But Nate did not need to track them. The warriors had been heading south toward Comanche territory since they left the spring.

Night fell, temporarily ending the pursuit. Nate had to settle for a cold camp; nothing was dry enough to burn. Jerky tided him over.

Daybreak was unusually cold for that time of year. Nate was covered with goose bumps when he headed out. He did not stay covered long. The rising sun brought rising temperatures and by midmorning once again he was sweltering.

Circling buzzards drew Nate's interest, but they were to the east, not the south. He was inclined to discount them and rode another half mile before common sense caused him to rein east.

Some of the buzzards scattered at his approach. Others went on feeding.

Nate took one look and was sick. Violently sick. It was worse than the husband, worse than any butchery, ever. He had to avert his gaze from what was left of her in order to do what he had to do. He nudged the remains into the shallow grave, tamped the mound of dirt, and folded his hands.

"The Lord is my shepherd, I shall not want," Nate began, and recited the rest of Psalm 23. It was all his numbed brain could think of.

Nate walked to the bay, reached for the reins, and paused. Here it was. The decision. North toward Bent's Fort or south and deeper into Comanche Grass?

Nate did not owe the Beechers. Not *this*, he didn't. He thought of Winona, his wife, and Evelyn, his daughter, and Zach, his son, and he climbed on the bay and reined to the south.

"We are being followed," Soko announced.

Pahkah and Sargento drew rein as Soko had done and turned to gaze intently along their back trail.

"I see no one," Sargento said.

"There was dust," Soko assured him.

"There is none now."

"I think it is one man," Soko said. "He stalks us."

The idea of someone hunting *them* was so extraordinary that neither Pahkah nor Sargento could hide his skepticism.

"We are at peace with the Cheyenne and the Arapaho," Pahkah mentioned. "Who else would dare?"

"The Utes would dare, but they seldom venture

this far out on the prairie," Soko said. "I believe it is a white man."

At this, Sargento indulged in a rare laugh. "Whites only hunt us in packs. You know that."

"Normally that is so," Soko agreed. "But a warrior from another tribe would not let us see his dust. That this man did, however little, tells me he is a white man." He lifted his reins. "I will go kill him."

"All of us will go," Pahkah said.

"No. He is following our dust. The two of you will go on and he will follow you. I will swing around behind him and take him by surprise."

Any argument the others might have offered was nipped by the jab of Soko's heels. He rode east at a slow walk so as not to raise dust of his own, avoiding tracts where the grass was particularly thin. When he had gone far enough not to be seen by whoever was shadowing them, he reined in a wide loop that should bring him up on the stalker's rear. It worked. The ground was hard, but there were partial tracks here and there, tracks made by a shod horse.

"It *is* a white man," Soko said, and smiled. It pleased him to have Sargento and Pahkah proven wrong. He hefted his war club but continued at a walk. He would wait until evening to move in close. The white man might have a rifle.

The sun climbed but a short way when Soko reined up in surprise. Ahead stood a horse. Not just any horse. The bay he and his friends had chased. Its reins dangled and it was cropping grass.

Soko's every nerve tingled. Something was not right. It must belong to the white man, but the white man would not go off and leave it. Yet that appeared to be what the white man had done. The ground was flat, the grass no more than knee-high and sparse. There was nowhere the white man could hide.

Still, Soko stayed where he was. His instincts warned him not to go nearer. Then the bay moved and Soko saw how it limped. Apparently, something was wrong with its front leg.

Soko thought he understood. The horse had gone lame and the white man had gone on, on foot. Soko kneed his mount forward. The bay raised its head and looked at him but showed no alarm and did not run off. He wondered if maybe the leg would heal and then the bay could be his, as fine an animal as any Nemene owned.

Soko was thinking of the bay when the grass broke apart and the white man rose up out of the earth and a sharp, penetrating pain filled Soko's belly even as he was torn from his horse and thrown to the ground. He lost his grip on the war club, but he still had his knife and would have grabbed for it except that the pain bent him in half. It was worse than any pain he'd ever felt. He tried to suppress it but could not.

His knife was plucked from its sheath.

Gasping for breath, Soko looked up. The white

man was big and broad-shouldered and bearded and held a folding knife coated with blood. *His* blood, dripping from the knife and from the white man's hand.

"How?" Soko marveled. "How did you kill me?"

The white man astounded him then. The white man spoke to him in the language of the Nemene. "I put a stone in the hoof of my horse to make it limp."

"But how did you hide in plain sight?"

The white man moved to where the grass had broken apart. He lifted a section of sod almost as long as he was tall and made a chopping motion with the knife.

Soko understood. The man had cut large pieces of sod, scattered the dirt under it, then covered himself with the sod as with a blanket and waited for a fly to ride into his web. It was clever. It was brilliant. "You have a name, white man?"

"Grizzly Killer."

"Why do you hunt us?"

"You killed the woman and her mate."

"How is it you speak the Nemene tongue?"

"I am an adopted Shoshone. The Shoshone tongue and the Nemene tongue are much alike. It is said that once the Nemene were Shoshone. That the Nemene drifted south and stayed and became a separate tribe but to this day the two tongues are very much alike."

"Our elders tell us the same," Soko said, with great effort.

"That makes us brothers."

His brow beaded with sweat, his teeth clenched against the torment, Soko smiled. "The only true brother a man has is himself." The world was growing dark, yet the sun was high in the sky.

"I have a water skin."

"No. But thank you." Soko gazed down at the gore and his intestines. "I did not expect it to be like this."

"We never do," Grizzly Killer said.

Soko shuddered uncontrollably.

"I can end it quickly if the pain is too much."

"I do not have long left," Soko said. The darkness was increasing. Already the sky was a dark brown and the white man a shadowy shape.

"Your friends will join you soon."

"One of us has gone on ahead with his dead brother," Soko said. "The white woman stabbed him."

"This I did not know," Grizzly Killer said.

The darkness was complete but Soko could still hear. "Will you hunt him as well?"

The answer was a while coming.

"No."

"You are an honorable enemy," Soko said, and died.

Nate King now had two horses, a war club, a knife, and the folding knife. He rode the bay and led the dead warrior's horse. He was not in any hurry. The china pitcher and the washbasin were not going anywhere. They would be at the trading post when he went to collect them.

Nate had found himself liking the Comanche he slew, but that did not change anything. Nothing short of his own death would stop him. He reckoned the other two Comanches would keep on south, expecting their friend to slay him before the day was out. They would not suspect anything was amiss.

The sun, the heat, and more miles of eating dust made for a long afternoon. He stopped often to rest the bay.

Nate had never been this far south on the prairie. So his surprise was that much greater when, late in the afternoon, the plain sloped gradually to a rise that overlooked a verdant valley. Approximately four miles long and maybe half that wide, the valley could harbor an entire village. The tracks of the two Comanches led into it, and smoke rose from amid the trees.

Nate dipped below the rise and circled to the west. He debated letting well enough alone and lighting a shuck for Bent's Fort. If there was a village, going after the two warriors would only get him killed.

But he had come this far.

He would not quit.

A coulee that fed into the stream was as good a spot as any to lie low until dark. Nate picketed the horses and stretched out in some shade. He could use the rest. He needed to have his wits about him later.

The sun was about to set when Nate woke up. He stretched, treated himself to pemmican, and walked the horses down the coulee to the stream. After they slaked their thirst, he led them back up the coulee and tethered them so they would not wander off.

Nate turned and took several steps, and changed his mind. Leaving the bay, he led the warhorse to the stream, climbed on, and rode east along the bank. In the twilight, from a distance—provided he kept his chin tucked to his chest so his short beard was not visible—he might pass for a returning warrior.

The Comanche's knife was in his own sheath, the war club in his right hand. Primitive by white standards, the club was nonetheless a superbly effective weapon in close combat. He should know. He had lost count of the number of enemy warriors who had tried to dash his brains out with one.

The woodland that bordered the stream lay quiet under the descending pall of night. The small birds that had been flitting about all day were now in their nests and roosts. Small game had sought haven from nocturnal predators. It seemed he had the woods to himself, but in the wild, as in civilization, appearances were deceiving.

Nate smelled smoke long before he spotted the flames that produced it in the middle of a clearing. He brought the horse to a halt and probed with all his senses. Tranquility seemingly reigned.

But the fire had not kindled itself.

The two warriors, and possibly others, could be anywhere.

Nate resorted to a ruse he had learned from the Shoshones. Gigging the horse toward the campfire, he swung onto its off-side and clung by an elbow and an ankle to give the illusion the horse was without a rider. From under its neck he sought sign of an ambush, but the horse advanced unmolested to the edge of the clearing, then stopped of its own accord.

Nate hung on, waiting for something to happen. No shouts arose. No flurry of feet greeted him. Yet the Comanches had to know the horse was there.

Nate had thought to catch them off-guard, to have them walk up to the horse to catch hold of the reins, only to be met by his war club and his knife. But no one was at the fire. No one was in the clearing.

There could only be one explanation.

Nate let go and dropped. As he did an arrow streaked out of the gloom. The tip that should have imbedded itself in his back instead imbedded itself in the horse. Rearing in pain, the animal whinnied, then fled across the clearing, the feathers jutting from its shoulder.

Nate had not meant for the horse to be hurt, but

he could do nothing to help it. Scrambling onto all fours, he plunged into the underbrush. It was well he did, for another shaft bit into the dirt exactly where he had landed.

Movement registered out of the corner of Nate's eye. He flattened a heartbeat before an arrow whizzed overhead. Scuttling low to the ground, he came to a log, slid up and over, and froze.

The Comanches did not come after him. They were seasoned warriors, and too savvy.

Nate's blood roared through his veins. It had been a close thing. Much too close. The pair had not fallen for his trick. Now it was him against them and they had the edge. Two against one, and they had better weapons.

Before the night was out, he might well be dead.

Sargento was mad. That they had missed once could be excused. But to miss with a second arrow, and then once more, was inexcusable. As an archer he had few peers, and Pahkah was almost as skilled. The dark was a factor, and the tangle of vegetation, but he was still mad. He had loosed two of the shafts himself.

Sargento's anger at himself was compounded by his anger over Soko. The older warrior had always been friendly to him, unlike some of the others. Since the white man was there and Soko was not, it left but one conclusion. The white man had killed Soko. All the more incentive for Sargento and Pahkah to kill the white man.

Staying low, Sargento glided nigh-soundlessly through the vegetation. He was unsure where the white man had gotten to but confident he would spot the white before the white spotted him. Sargento had hunted whites before and they were ridiculously easy to kill. Almost as easy as Mexicans. Sargento held both in the highest contempt. With few exceptions, their skill as warriors was laughable. The reason the whites had exterminated so many tribes lay in their numbers and their guns, not in their prowess as warriors.

The thought of guns caused Sargento to go slower. The white man was bound to have a rifle and pistol. It surprised Sargento a little that the man had not fired at them. That was the first reaction on every white's part. Shoot in a panic, and miss. But this one had not panicked, had not wasted a bullet. It hinted he might be more cautious than most of his kind.

Sargento had lost sight of Pahkah. The other warrior was somewhere to his right, no doubt searching for the white even as he was doing. If things went as they should, they would catch the white man between them.

Time passed. Sargento stopped beside a tree, his brow furrowed. There had not been any sign of his quarry. It was most strange. He was about to move on when Pahkah crept out of the brush to his side. Pahkah's brow, too, was puckered in puzzlement.

It was too dark for sign talk so Pahkah whispered. "I do not like this. He has vanished."

"He is probably lying on his belly somewhere shaking with fear," Sargento said.

"Not this one," Pahkah disagreed. "He rode to the clearing on Soko's horse. Fear is not in him."

"He is white," Sargento said.

"Did you not see? He wears buckskins."

"So? A lot of whites wear buckskins and they are no more formidable than fleas."

"Some of the buckskins live with Indians. Some take Indian wives. They are not sheep like most whites. They are wolves."

Sargento had not thought of that. It *would* take considerable skill to best a wily warrior like Soko. "You have a suggestion?"

"One of us will lure him out of hiding and the other will be ready to slay him," Pahkah proposed.

"Who does the luring and who does the slaying?"

"Since it is my idea, I will be the bait. You know what to do." Without another word Pahkah stalked toward the clearing, a shadow among shadows, only this time he made more noise than he ordinarily would. The rustle of a bush here, the scrape of a leaf there. Enough to make it seem natural.

Sargento followed, the string to his bow pulled halfway back. He must be ready. He must let fly in the blink of an eye and he must not miss. He saw that Pahkah was stopping every few strides to present a tempting target.

Sargento admired the other's bravery. It took great courage to dare a blast from the white's gun. Determined not to let any harm come to him, Sargento marked every shadow, every possible point of ambush. But nothing happened. The white man did not appear. No shots boomed in the dark.

Pahkah came to within a few steps of the clearing, and hunkered. He was rubbing his chin when Sargento came up to him.

"I do not understand."

"You are not alone," Sargento admitted.

"Where *is* he?" Pahkah whispered.

"This time I will be the one to lure him out. I will go to the stream. You follow, but not too near."

"I will be ready."

Sargento did as Pahkah had done, moving stealthily but not so stealthily the white man would fail to spot him. The skin between his shoulder blades crawled. He fully expected the white man to shoot him in the back. Such cowardly acts were typical of his kind. But again no shots crackled. Again, the white man did not show himself.

More perplexed than ever, Sargento came to the bank, and stopped.

Soon Pahkah joined him. "Maybe the white man has gone. Maybe our arrows put fear into him."

Sargento grunted. "It does not take much to put fear into a white. I only had to hold my knife next to the neck of the woman with the yellow hair and she could not stop screaming."

"We will wait until daylight and hunt him" Pahkah said. "He will not escape us."

"We should hide our horses before he decides to come back and steal them," Sargento advised.

That is what they did. They crept to the clearing, quietly mounted, and rode east side by side.

As they passed under an oak, Sargento's mount pricked its ears and raised its head. Sargento snapped his own head up in time to glimpse something launch itself from an overspreading bough.

"Above us!"

The white man dropped between them. He had a knife in one hand and a war club in the other, and he struck at both of them as he dropped.

Pain exploded in Sargento's shoulder, courtesy of the war club. He threw himself from the other side of his horse and alighted like a cat on the balls of his feet. He looked to put a shaft into the white man, but the white man was not there. Only Pahkah, lying still, limbs akimbo, the hilt of a knife sticking from his chest.

Sargento was stunned. It had been so quick. He turned right and then left. A shadow moved, and the bow was knocked from his hands. Grabbing for his knife, he attacked. He ducked a swing of the war club, speared the knife out. The white man dodged. He evaded a thrust and stabbed low, only to have the blade deflected by the war club. Feinting at the white man's gut, he lanced the tip of the blade at the man's throat. It was a move he had used before, a move that never failed him. Somehow the white man avoided it.

The war club was a blur. More pain racked Sargento's left knee. His leg buckled and he stumbled. Before he could recover, pain burst in his right knee. He tried to straighten but his legs would not work. He looked up and saw the war club arc toward his head.

It cannot end like this! Sargento frantically told himself. *Not at the hands of a white man!*

The next explosion of pain brought a flood of white light followed by a plunge into the inkiest blackness.

Sargento's last thought was that this was a stupid way to die.

CHAPTER TWELVE

The whiskey did it.

One-Eye Jackson planned to pass on by Bent's Fort. He had plenty of supplies, what with the packhorse he had stolen from the Beechers. He had an extra rifle and extra pistols, the weapons he had taken from Nate King. He had no reason at all to stop at the trading post on his way to the mountains. No reason at all except for the whiskey.

One-Eye had a fondness for red-eye. He liked whiskey like some men liked women. He had the sense not to indulge when he was in the wilds, but whenever he stopped at a frontier outpost he made up for lost opportunity.

So it was the whiskey that brought One-Eye to Bent's. The whiskey, and the extra horses, the mounts belonging to Shipley and Cynthia. One-

Eye figured they would fetch a nice price. Money he could convert to more whiskey before setting out for the high country.

One-Eye had been at the post half an hour, ensconced in a shaded corner where he could drink in peace. He had downed half the bottle, which for him was barely enough to whet his thirst. He was tipping the bottle for another long swig when an individual he had never much cared for came striding toward him.

Ceran St. Vrain, as aristocratic as ever, with two hirelings in two, made no pretense at friendliness. "You again."

One-Eye finished his swig and wiped his mouth with his sleeve. "I never have savvied why you dislike me so."

"Let me see. You are a liar, a cheat, and a thief. Half the mountain men despise you and the rest would as soon gut you as look at you. The Shoshones say you are bad medicine and have spread word to the other tribes to have nothing to do with you. I would say that is ample reason enough."

One-Eye smirked. "So long as I don't lie, cheat, or steal within these walls, I'm free to come and go as I please. That is your rule, isn't it?"

"It is," St. Vrain acknowledged.

"As for the Injuns," One-Eye said, "I'm not the only white they won't have any truck with."

"True. But the fact remains, you are the least liked white man of anyone I know, and it would please me greatly if you were to step over the line so I can ban you from the premises."

"I'm plumb sorry to disappoint you," One-Eye said sarcastically.

St. Vrain turned to go and his gaze alighted on the horses. "I say," he remarked. "That packhorse looks familiar. As I recall, you did not have a pack animal when you left here."

"I bought it," One-Eye lied. "Paid forty dollars in coin."

"From whom?"

"I don't see as how that's any of your business," One-Eye hedged.

"Do you have a bill of sale?"

"Who the hell bothers with stuff like that way out here?" One-Eye angrily answered. "They wanted forty dollars and I paid them forty dollars and that was it."

"They?"

"What?"

"You said they, as in plural." St. Vrain studied the horse and the packs closely. "If only I could remember where I've seen this animal before."

"Go remember somewhere else," One-Eye said. "I have serious drinking to do, and I don't need you putting a damper on things." He chugged more whiskey, watching through slitted lids as St. Vrain made for the other end of the post. "Snootier-than-thou," he growled, but only after St. Vrain was out of earshot.

One-Eye was happy to note that no one else

had showed any interest. But the packhorse started to worry him. If St. Vrain nearly recognized it, others might, too. They might remember the young farmer and his wife, and wonder what he was doing with their animal.

One-Eye reluctantly corked the whiskey and placed the bottle in a pack. For the moment he would forget about selling the two horses. Maybe it was for the best, he told himself. He was still on good terms with the Crows. He could parley the horses into permission to stay with the Crows a spell, and possibly have a woman thrown into the barter.

The reins to his mount in one hand and the lead rope to the rest of the horses in the other, One-Eye made for the wide gate in the middle of the south wall. He was not all that eager to leave. But sometimes a man had to cut and run or be cut down by circumstances over which he had no control.

The post was doing a bustling business. Indians were present: some Cheyenne, several Nez Perce, a pair of Flatheads. A freight train bound for Santa Fe was leaving in the hour and the freighters were scurrying about like so many ants. The few frontiersmen he saw were strangers.

One-Eye halted at the gate and hollered for it to be opened. In his opinion it was a damned nuisance, how it was always kept closed. "Move a little slower, why don't you?" he complained when the men responsible did not open it fast enough to suit him.

"Keep your britches on, mister," was the peckish reply.

Irritated, One-Eye uncorked the bottle and tilted it to his mouth. He watched the amber liquor to see how much he could drain in one gulp. The level dropped nearly half an inch. Belching, he lowered the bottle and stared out the open gate—and found his way barred by the last person on the planet he wanted to meet up with. "It can't be!" he blurted.

"Going somewhere?" Nate King asked. He had heard Jackson bellow for the gate to be opened as he rode up, and had unslung the bow he had taken from one of the dead Comanches.

Any other time, Nate would have been amused by the amazement on Jackson's face. But now he felt only simmering rage that burned like a red-hot ember deep inside him.

The whiskey bottle hit the ground and shattered. Jackson glanced down in surprise, then gaped at Nate. "You made it back alive!"

"No thanks to you," Nate said. "But the rest are all dead. The farmer. His wife. The Comanches."

"You killed the Comanches?" Jackson said in blatant fear. His good eye darted right and left. He resembled, more than anything, a weasel backed into a corner.

"One more to go," Nate said, "and I can go home."

"Do you mean me?" Jackson nervously asked, and laughed a brittle laugh. "Have you forgotten the rules? No blood is to be spilled in the post. Ever. Anyone who breaks the rule will be banned for life."

"It's worth it."

"St. Vrain and the Bents are your friends. You wouldn't want to cross them, would you?"

"Root hog or die where you stand," Nate said. "I don't care which."

Jackson fingered his belt and glanced at his horse. The butt of his rifle poked from out of his bedroll. The butt of another rifle—Nate's Hawken—jutted from a pack on the packhorse.

"Don't take all day making up your mind," Nate said.

They were blocking the gate. People were staring, pointing, whispering.

The men who had opened the gate were listening to the exchange. One started toward them, but the other gripped his arm and said, "No, boyo. Let them settle it between themselves."

"It's not fair," One-Eye said. "You don't care if you get banned but I do."

"You're stalling," Nate said. "And you're taking it for granted you will leave here alive."

"I must admit," One-Eye grinned, "I fully intend to."

"Start the quadrille whenever you are ready."

Jackson laughed and started to turn, but it was a ruse. His hands swooped to his pistols and he jerked them clear of his belt.

Nate was faster. He was no Robin Hood, but neither was he completely without experience with a bow. From friends among the Shoshones he had learned the basic skills needed. Touch The Clouds had tutored him in the finer points in exchange for lessons in how to fire a gun. That tutoring served Nate in critical stead, for as Jackson's pistols leveled, Nate loosed a shaft.

The barbed tip transfixed One-Eye's shoulder. Jackson shrieked, staggered, and fled toward the blacksmith shop. He fired as he ran, but his aim was off. Lead whistled over Nate's head.

Shouts erupted. People scurried for cover. It was common knowledge that innocent bystanders had a habit of taking stray slugs.

Jackson disappeared into the blacksmith's. There was a sharp yell and the sound of a blow. The blacksmith stumbled out, blood streaming from a head wound, and collapsed.

Vaulting from the saddle, Nate ran to a freight wagon parked near the shop. The thin metal rim on a wheel was being replaced, and had been partially removed. Ducking behind the wagon, Nate peered between the spokes. The anvil was visible, and so was a workbench. But the forge at the back and the rest of the interior were mired in shadow.

From out of that shadow came a snarl. "Damn

you! I've broken off the tip, but I can't get it out! I'll kill you for this, King. So help me God, this is your last day on earth." More swearing punctuated the threat.

Nate said nothing. To talk in battle was the height of folly. He must stay focused.

"Come and get me, big man! I can't wait to blow out your wick!"

Nate glanced at the packhorse. He would fare better with his Hawken, but Jackson was probably expecting him to try for it and would cut him down before he reached it.

"What's the matter?" One-Eye taunted. "Nothing to say now that it's come to a showdown?"

Bent low, Nate darted around the front of the wagon toward the shop. He angled to the right and had covered half the distance when a shot boomed and his left leg was knocked out from under him. As he fell he sent a shaft streaking at a wreath of smoke. Then, scrambling erect, he hopped like mad on his good leg. He came to the open door and leaned against it, taking stock.

The slug had ripped a furrow in his calf but had not severed a blood vessel or nicked the bone. His leg would heal, given time. Provided he lived.

"Still with me, King?" One-Eye cackled. "Maybe bleeding to death, I hope?"

Nate notched another arrow. Jackson had changed position and was over at the far side. Nate had visited the shop before, and remembered bins of scrap metal and coal and firewood lining the wall. Perfect cover from arrow or bullet.

"Come on, talk to me!" One-Eye shouted. "It's not like I don't know where you are and you don't know where I am."

"I can't wait for you to breathe your last."

"That's the spirit! But you're getting ahead of yourself. I don't die easy. Just ask your Shoshone friends."

"This is for the Beechers," Nate said.

"So she got to you, did she? That little blond vixen with the straying eyes? I can't say as I blame you. She was as pretty a piece of fluff as ever I've laid eyes on. But I can't say much for her choice in men."

Nate was in motion while Jackson was still talking. He sank to his knees behind the base on which the anvil rested.

A pistol cracked, but the shot was a shade too slow.

Jackson, surprisingly, seemed unconcerned. "Tricky devil, aren't you?" he said from somewhere near the bins.

Drawing the string back to his cheek, Nate peered past the anvil. Instantly a flintlock spat lead and flame, and a puff of air fanned his ear. Nate let the shaft fly and heard it *thwack* into the wall. He had missed, or Jackson had changed position yet again.

It was the latter, as another mocking snicker

proved. "Is that the best you can do, Grizzly Killer? You're not much shakes with a bow, are you?"

Jackson was crawling toward the furnace, Nate suspected. Swiftly nocking another arrow, he sighted along it at a patch of shadow lighter than the rest. He waited, holding his breath to steady his aim, but Jackson did not appear.

Again a pistol boomed. The slug spanged off the anvil inches from Nate's face. He instinctively ducked as slivers stung his cheek and neck.

A shrill laugh came out of the depths of the shop. "Almost snuffed your wick that time."

Nate reached for the quiver. He had one arrow left. Nocking it, he drew on the string. Comanche bows were powerful, strong enough to send an arrow into the heart of a buffalo. The strain on his upper arm and shoulders was considerable. He sought some suggestion of movement, but there was none.

A shape heaved up near the furnace. Without thinking, Nate sighted and released, and even as he did, he saw that the shape was not a man but a stool that Jackson had flung.

Nate whirled as his nemesis came charging around the anvil. Jackson pointed a pistol at his head. In reflex, Nate threw the bow. It struck Jackson's wrist at the moment Jackson fired. The shot went wild.

Lunging, Nate seized Jackson's wrists. He swung Jackson against the anvil with bone-jarring force and the pistol clattered to the ground.

Snarling, One-Eye wrenched free. The hand that had held the pistol suddenly held a knife.

Nate's own palm molded around the hilt of the knife he had taken from the Comanche. He avoided a stab at his heart, sidestepped a slash at his arm. His own cut at Jackson's neck missed. One-Eye immediately sheared at his groin.

Twisting, Nate backpedaled. He collided with the anvil. His ankle caught and he fell. Flailing for something to hold on to, he slammed his hand against the anvil and lost his hold on the knife.

One-Eye Jackson loomed above him. His mouth curled in vicious glee, he swept his own knife overhead. "I've got you now, you son of a bitch."

Nate's groping hand closed on a long handle. He swung it at Jackson's leg, not knowing what it was, and heard the crunch of knee cartilage. Jackson howled and tottered, and Nate pushed to his feet. He saw what he held, the blacksmith's big hammer. He swung it as he rose, catching Jackson in the side. Ribs cracked and snapped, and One-Eye folded in half, screeching oaths.

Nate's right arm described a circle. The head of the hammer and Jackson's head met, and the softer yielded to the harder with a loud *splat*.

Nate stared a moment, then dropped the gore-spattered hammer and limped slowly out into the sunlight. Scores of onlookers hung back as he limped to the packhorse and reclaimed his Hawken and his pistols. He was rummaging in the packs for his bowie and his tomahawk when footsteps came up behind him.

"He's dead, I take it?"

"As dead as they get," Nate said. He found his bowie, slid it into his sheath, and turned.

"Good riddance. But this puts me in a bind," Ceran St. Vrain said. "We have rules, you know. One of them is that anyone guilty of taking a life within the confines of these walls is subject to banishment."

"Do what you have to."

St. Vrain nodded. "I hereby banish you, then. For fifteen minutes. After that you are free to come and go as you please."

Nate wearily smiled.

"I'll have food brought to my quarters. See you there in a quarter of an hour." St. Vrain went to walk off, then stopped and snapped his fingers. "That reminds me. Do you still want that pitcher and washbasin? I found them in Bent's office after you left."

Nate did not have to think about it. "No."

"Pardon me?"

"They would always remind me. Order a new set. A set that won't be tainted by the horror."

"I am not sure I understand but I will do as you request."

"Thank you, Ceran."

"You sure have gone to a lot of trouble, old friend."

"They call it love," Nate said.

"Is there anything else I can get for you?"

Nate King grinned. "Brandy. Lots and lots of brandy."

#50
WILDERNESS
PEOPLE OF THE FOREST
SPECIAL GIANT EDITION!
David Thompson

When Nate King chose a new valley in which to build his home, he wanted to get away from all civilization and the inevitable trouble it brings. But Nate can't duck trouble for very long. A hostile band of Indians has also laid claim to the Kings' valley, and they've made it clear they're not willing to share. In a desperate act to punish Nate and his family, they capture his daughter, Evelyn. And Nate will do anything it takes—even if it means sacrificing his own life—to get her back.

#49
WILDERNESS
WOLVERINE
David Thompson

In the harsh wilderness of the Rocky Mountains, every day presents a new challenge. Nate King and his family have survived by overcoming those challenges, one by one. But in the new valley that is their home, they face perils they've never before known. Some of the most vicious predators on the continent are stalking the Kings and their friends. Nate has gone up against grizzlies, mountain lions, and enraged buffalo, but he's never battled wolverines—cunningly savage killers that know no fear. One wolverine is dangerous enough, but five live in this valley…and they're out for blood.

ZANE GREY®

CABIN GULCH

In a fit of anger, Joan Randle sends Jim Cleve into the untamed mining camps of Idaho Territory to prove his grit and spirit. Then she regrets their quarrel and sets off after him to bring him back. But she crosses the path of Jack Kells, the notorious mining camp and stagecoach bandit, who captures her and intends to keep her as his woman. He is willing to kill two of his own men to have her all to himself, so how can Joan hope to escape? Her hopes will fade even more when Jim Cleve shows up—and joins Kells' gang....

RAIN VALLEY

LAURAN PAINE

Lauran Paine is one of the West's most powerful storytellers. In the title novella of this collection, Burt Crownover causes quite a stir when he steals into Rain Valley in the middle of the night. It's no surprise the ranchers are suspicious. They've got a herd of highly valuable cattle and any stranger could be a thief. But is Burt a rustler out to con them, or just the man they need to help protect their stock?

Dorchester Publishing Co., Inc.
P.O. Box 6640   ___5783-2
Wayne, PA 19087-8640 $5.99 US/$7.99 CAN
Please add $2.50 for shipping and handling for the first book and $.75 for each additional book.
NY and PA residents, add appropriate sales tax. No cash, stamps, or CODs. Canadian orders
require $2.00 for shipping and handling and must be paid in U.S. dollars. Prices and availability
subject to change. **Payment must accompany all orders.**

Name: _____

Address: _____

City: _____ State: _____ Zip: _____

E-mail: _____

I have enclosed $_____ in payment for the checked book(s).

CHECK OUT OUR WEBSITE! www.dorchesterpub.com
____ Please send me a free catalog.

WILL HENRY

BLIND CAÑON

In the midst of the Alaskan gold rush, Murrah Starr holds a rich claim that should set him up for life. Trouble is, his life may be a lot shorter than he'd like. Starr is a half-breed Sioux whose only friend is a wolf dog he once freed from a trap. Angus McClennon, the head of the local miners' association, is dead set on taking Starr's claim for himself. First he spearheads a law that declares only American citizens can own a mine. Then a group of miners beat Starr and leave him for dead in the middle of the street. But Starr is just as determined as McClennon. He's determined to fight for what's his—and to stay alive while doing it!